ALPHA DRAGON'S EAGLE

The Dragonfate Games Book 2

HAWKE OAKLEY

❀ Created with Vellum

ONE

Thystle

As the final song on the album faded out, a tear sprang to my eye.

I took a deep breath as I opened my eyes to stare at the ceiling. My soul felt raw and exposed, but full. TalonStorm made me feel *alive* like no other band did.

I wiped the tear away and sat up in bed. Even though the CD had run its course, waiting for me to replay it, that didn't mean TalonStorm was far. All four of my walls were plastered with posters featuring the band members, although one in particular stood out.

Aquila.

I couldn't think about him without my heart skipping a beat. He was perfect in every way. The sway of his hips on stage flustered me, and his voice turned my knees to jelly.

And then there were his eyes—the only part of him that wasn't covered up by an elaborate bird mask.

They were a magnetic, earthy shade of brown, like roasted amber. I stared at them, spellbound. I could only look at him in the poster like this when I wasn't listening to

1

his music. If I did both at the same time, I got overwhelmed, like staring directly into the sun.

Putting the CD player aside, I sat on my knees and gazed up at the big poster above my headboard. My hand reached out to touch it, running down Aquila's masked face, down his chest... then I pulled my hand away before I went any lower. I was too shy to touch him like that, even in the privacy of my bedroom.

That wasn't to say I didn't *think* about touching him at night under the covers...

I sighed and rested my head against the wall, my cheek touching the cool glossy paper. Being so close to Aquila—even this printed likeness of him—made my heart race. He was the perfect omega—talented, handsome, kind to his fans.

Of which, I was number one, obviously.

But he didn't even know I existed. And more than anything in the world, I wished he did.

Nobody else understood. My brothers teased me over it. I was just a teenage alpha dragon living on some random island in the middle of nowhere. Meanwhile, Aquila was a superstar. He was the vocalist in the most popular band of our time, TalonStorm. Despite being a shifter group, they were beloved among humans, too. They kept their animal identities a secret, too, which gave them an extra air of mystery. Fans flocked to him every time Aquila appeared in public, and TalonStorm's shows always sold out within minutes.

Since I wasn't allowed to leave the island, I'd never been to one of their concerts before. But that was about to change.

My seventeenth birthday was in a week, and TalonStorm's next ticket sale was on the exact same day.

It was literally fate. It *had* to be.

I'd convince my brother, Cobalt, I was responsible enough to go if it was the last thing I did.

A rush of determination launched me to my feet. I grabbed my CD player as a comfort item, then marched down the hall to Cobalt's room. As the oldest, he got a big room in a separate wing of the castle.

My heart hammered anxiously. What if he said no? He couldn't. There was no way. I may have been young, but I wasn't as irresponsible as my stupid twin brothers. Cobalt couldn't lump me in with them, even if we were close in age.

But deep down, I was nervous. Cobalt was so serious that he was hard to read sometimes.

I took a breath. I had to believe in myself. Cobalt was stern, but fair. If I made my case well, he'd have to agree.

And besides, this was fate. He couldn't say no to fate.

Clutching the CD player to my chest, I stood at Cobalt's massive door. My nerves were a jumbled mess in my chest, and my stomach felt like a heaving mess of worms.

Everything rode on this. If my brother refused, my whole life would be ruined.

I closed my eyes and pictured Aquila.

You can do it, Thystle, imaginary Aquila told me, flashing me that gorgeous smile.

I instantly felt better. He was right. I'd do it—for him.

"Trying to introduce Cobalt to TalonStorm?"

I jumped at Jade's voice behind me. If it was Aurum or Saffron, I would've bristled at their interruption, but Jade was fine. Out of my six brothers, he was among the least irritating.

I huffed. "No."

"Ah." He tilted his head and pushed his glasses up. "Something else?"

I shuffled on my feet. Would Jade help my case if I told him the truth? He was older than me, so he had more seniority, and next to Cobalt, he was the most responsible.

"I... I need to ask Cobalt something," I admitted.

Jade's thin brows rose. "Oh? It sounds serious."

"It is."

A low snort came from nearby. My guard went up as Crimson strolled into view and stood next to Jade. He wore a brand-new suit that he was clearly showing off. He had nothing better to do than walk around and gloat about his dumb hoard.

"Thystle is a sixteen-year-old dragon who gets everything he wants," Crimson prattled. "How serious can it be?"

Jade shot him a wry glance. "You were sixteen once, too. Don't you remember how important everything felt back then?"

A rush of anger seared inside me. I hated when my older brothers talked about me like I wasn't there. I clutched my CD player tighter. My claws threatened to burst out of my skin, but I kept them in check to protect my comfort item.

"Don't you have a suit to have sex with?" I spat to Crimson.

He scoffed. "I would *never* sully my hoard like that."

"Whatever, just go away!"

"Touchy," Crimson grumbled.

"I'll take care of this," Jade said, gently urging Crimson to go the fuck away.

Fortunately, Crimson got the hint.

"Good luck," he said to Jade under his breath before striding down the hall to show off his new suit to anyone who gave a shit—which was nobody.

But Crimson's comments soured my mood and raised

my hackles. Who was he to judge how serious my problems were? He still thought of me as a dumb, ignorant kid.

What if Cobalt did, too?

My anxiety worsened. My talk with Cobalt *had* to go well. There was no other option.

"Don't mind him," Jade said, composed as ever. I didn't know how he did that. Staying calm under any circumstance was like his superpower. "Do you want to talk it out?"

I chewed my lip. Crimson had shot my nerves, so now even speaking to Jade felt like a challenge. But if I couldn't even tell Jade, the least judgmental of my brothers, how could I face Cobalt?

Once again, I pictured Aquila's hand on my shoulder, reassuring me. It gave me the strength I needed.

"I'm going to ask Cobalt's permission to leave the island," I said. "So I can see TalonStorm in concert." Jade's eyes widened slightly before returning to normal. "I see."

His lack of reaction made me nervous. That could've meant anything.

"Well, I know how important they are to you," Jade said. "It's worth asking."

My spirits rose, if only a little. A gentle nudge in Cobalt's direction was better than nothing.

Jade wished me luck and left me alone. I mustered my courage and knocked on the massive door.

A chill ran down my spine when Cobalt's deep voice replied, "Enter."

Keeping my CD player close, I walked into his room. Cobalt sat with his broad back to me as he stared out the long bay windows, watching the ocean waves.

"H-hey, Cobalt," I said.

It wasn't that I was afraid of Cobalt. He was my

5

protective older brother, and I knew he loved me. But he was so damned serious all the time, like a robot. I could never tell if he was in a good mood or a shitty one, which made it harder to plead my case.

"What brings you here, Thystle?" Cobalt asked without looking at me. His deep, rumbly voice filled the room like gravel.

My heart thumped. My nerves were so frayed I felt like I might shift out of instinct.

"I need to ask you something," I said.

Finally, Cobalt turned around to face me. His expression was completely neutral. "Tell me."

I swallowed the anxious lump in my throat.

I *had* to do this. For Aquila.

"My birthday is next week," I began.

Cobalt gave a slight nod.

I paused, hoping to put more emphasis on my words. "And, on the exact same day, TalonStorm tickets are going on sale."

My brother stared at me, stone-faced. I had no clue what he was thinking.

"So... I want to buy—no, I'm *going* to buy one," I stated. "I'm going to buy a ticket to their next concert." Cobalt stood up. A shiver ran down my spine.

"You intend to leave the island?" he asked. His tone was the same as it was two seconds ago, but it felt darker now.

But I couldn't back down. I'd come so far.

"Yes," I said, meeting his unblinking, dark blue eyes.

Cobalt walked closer, his every step sounding like an earthquake in the silence of his room. He towered over me, broad and tall. I stood my ground.

"You shouldn't go," Cobalt said.

My heart plummeted. That wasn't what I wanted to hear.

But I was also furious. He hadn't even heard me out!

I squared my shoulders. "Cobalt, listen. TalonStorm is my life. Music is my *hoard*. You know how important that is."

Cobalt stared, but I seized his silence as an invitation to continue.

"And the lead singer, Aquila—he's special to me. I've never felt like this for anybody before. I need this chance to see him in person," I pleaded. "He could be my fated mate!"

Cobalt's eyes flashed at that phrase. "You are young, Thystle. You can't know that."

Fury raged in my blood, setting it on fire.

"And you can't know that he's not!" I snarled.

We glared at each other. At least, I thought Cobalt was glaring. There was a sharp edge in his gaze that wasn't there a second ago.

"He is older than you," Cobalt said.

"Not by much," I argued. "Only six years. When I'm an adult, it won't make a difference."

"He doesn't know you."

"When I go to this concert, he will."

I didn't care if it sounded naive. It was how I really felt.

"Is he even an omega?" Cobalt asked.

"He says he is," I retorted.

"It could be a lie."

"Even if it's a lie, it doesn't matter. A couple doesn't need to be an alpha and an omega."

Cobalt was quiet for a while, staring at me with those blank, deep-sea creature eyes. The longer he stayed silent, the angrier I got. I was pissed—but more than that, I was scared. Scared of Cobalt shooting me down, refusing my request.

"You shouldn't leave the island," Cobalt warned. "Wait until you're older and stronger."

I shook my head vehemently. "I have to. For Talon-Storm. For Aquila."

"If Aquila truly is your fated mate, he will wait for you."

That was such an annoying argument. It pissed me off.

"I'm sick of you controlling everyone, Cobalt," I snapped. "I don't care anymore. I'm flying off the island to see TalonStorm, no matter what you say!"

Cobalt's face was a brick wall.

And then, he said the thing I dreaded the most.

"Viol didn't care, either. He left the island around your age. And look what happened to him. It *changed* him."

I couldn't argue with that. My rage deflated.

"I know," I mumbled.

Viol's incident was the reason us younger dragons couldn't leave the island. It wasn't fair.

"I know you're just trying to protect us," I said, looking up at my big brother. "But I want this *so* badly, Cobalt. Please try to understand me. I know I'm young, and you probably think this is a phase, but it's not." I clenched my heart. "Aquila and TalonStorm mean everything to me."

After a moment, Cobalt sighed and rolled up his sleeve. For a second, I thought he was gearing up to hit me for my insolence. Instead, he held his forearm in front of my face.

"If you are truly this dedicated," Cobalt said, "then show me with your fangs."

I gasped. I almost asked Cobalt if he was serious, but that was a stupid question. Cobalt was always serious.

I stared at his arm, ready for me.

I closed my eyes.

For Aquila.

The shift came to me like a shooting arrow, true and committed. It concentrated in my mouth so that the only part of me that shifted was my teeth. They elongated and sharpened into two rows of dragon fangs.

Fuelled by my obsession with Aquila, I sank my fangs into Cobalt's forearm.

He didn't even flinch. He stood as steady as a rock as blood ran down his skin. I didn't move, waiting for him to give me some kind of signal. My heart raced as I met his stoic gaze.

Finally, Cobalt smiled.

"All right, Thystle. You have my permission."

I was delirious with joy. I'd never been so happy in my life.

After getting his green light, I ran down the hall back to my room with a skip in my step. Even in my human form, I felt like I could fly.

When I reached my room, I threw myself onto my bed. I hugged the CD player with the TalonStorm album inside close to my chest, squishing it affectionately.

"I did it," I breathed. "I'm really gonna go!"

A burst of pure bliss made me kick my legs and laugh. I glanced backwards at the poster of Aquila hanging over my bed. He looked down at me proudly.

"I did it, Aquila," I breathed, tears brimming in my eyes. "Just wait. I'll see you soon."

"Who's laughing like a maniac in here?" Aurum asked as he strolled inside.

Crap. I'd run back to my room in such a hurry I forgot to shut the door. It didn't matter, though. Not even my most annoying brother could bring me down right now.

A second, similar voice joined Aurum's. Saffron gawked at me. "Whoa, is Thystle actually *smiling?*"

"And why's your mouth covered in blood?" Aurum asked. "Are you in, like, a vampire phase?"

The golden twins stood by the bed and exchanged a startled glance, as if me smiling was some freak occurrence.

Unlike any other time, I didn't even care that they were bugging me. I was too happy.

"Yeah, I'm smiling," I said wistfully, ignoring the blood comment.

Aurum snickered. "I didn't know goths could smile."

Since I was on cloud nine, I didn't bother correcting him for the billionth time that I was emo, not goth.

"Uh huh," I murmured, still grinning.

The twins shrugged at each other.

"Hey, uh, Thystle?" Saffron began. "Are you okay?"

"Mhm. I'm the best I've ever been," I said.

Hesitancy crept into Saffron's voice. "Uh, are you sure...?"

"Yeah, what's with you, dude?" Aurum chimed in.

I sat up, still holding my CD player close. My brothers looked unnerved at my unusually happy expression.

"Cobalt's letting me go see TalonStorm in concert," I told them.

I expected to see shock and jealousy on their faces. After all, they were still stuck here. But Aurum and Saffron almost looked sad.

"Hey, it's okay, guys," I reassured them. "If you wanna go somewhere, all you have to do is ask."

That didn't help. They were even more distressed and uncomfortable, like their dog died. And we didn't have a dog.

Saffron rubbed his arm. "Um, Thystle..."

He shot his twin a glance, as if wanting *him* to take over, but Aurum blanched like he was about to be sick.

"What's going on, you guys?" I asked.

Saffron winced. "Have you not heard?"

"No?"

Now I was starting to freak out. Why wouldn't they tell me what was going on?

"Did somebody get hurt? Is the island on fire?" I demanded.

"Thystle..." Saffron bit his lip. "TalonStorm broke up."

And with those three words, my life was ruined. Forever.

TWO

Thystle

Life was pain. Agony. Torture, even.

But my baby nephew was pretty darn cute.

Ever since my brother, Crimson, found his fated mate, Taylor, on the Dragonfate Games, my life had slightly improved. I never did meet my fated mate—as if it could've been anyone other than Aquila—but having an adorable, chubby little infant around was a definite plus.

But today was the ten-year anniversary of Talon-Storm's breakup, and despite all the time that'd passed, I was still as crushed now as I was back then.

I sighed as I lay in bed, staring up at the ceiling. The long bangs that usually covered one side of my face flopped limply back onto my pillow.

Ever since that day, I was stuck in a rut—and not the sexy kind. I felt stifled and restless, like there was no point to anything because TalonStorm didn't exist anymore. I knew that was a pointless, stupid way to feel, but it didn't stop the emotions from happening.

We dragons used "lizard brain" as an insult, but at

12

times like this, I wished I *did* have more of a lizard brain. Maybe then I wouldn't get sucked into my feelings all the time. How simple life would be if all I cared about were my next meal and finding a heat source...

My eyes strayed around my room. After that day, I lost my mind. It wasn't pretty. I cried. I screamed. I threw things. After my fit was over, I shut down. I was too heartbroken to find out what the hell happened. Why TalonStorm broke up. Aurum and Saffron offered to tell me rumors, but I didn't want to know the details. I just didn't care.

In my acute distress, I took down all my TalonStorm posters and eventually replaced them with other bands. I just couldn't handle seeing the posters and knowing they were gone.

But there was one poster I didn't touch—the one of Aquila above my bed.

I gazed up at him. The color had faded, and the corners of the paper had wrinkled over time, but the image of my favorite singer still affected me deeply. Whenever I felt bad, I'd look at him... and somehow, even though he was a 2D image printed on a piece of paper, he made it seem like everything would be okay.

After everything I went through to approach Cobalt that day, it was all for nothing. I never went to that concert, so I never left the island. There was no point. After TalonStorm broke up, nothing pulled me away. Aquila was still out there, but without concerts or signings or meet-and-greets, how would I ever find him?

I sighed harder, as if exhaling would expel these crappy feelings.

A knock came at the door. As usual, I wasn't in the mood for visitors. That was why I kept the damn door closed. But when Taylor's voice came from the other side, my irritation vanished. Where Taylor went, my nephew, Ruby, always followed. Even my legendary whinging couldn't stand up to the brute force of a cute baby.

"Hey, Thystle? Are you busy?" Taylor asked.

I sat up, my hair messily falling back into place. "No. Come in."

Taylor and Crimson slipped inside with Ruby in tow. I cracked a smile at the sight of my nephew. He plodded into my room in his human form, curiously gazing around with wide eyes. I was sure my bedroom, with all its colorful posters, was enthralling for a kid his age. Better than some other stuffy hoards, like Crimson's suits or Jade's books.

"Sorry for barging in like this," Taylor said as he followed Ruby around, making sure he didn't knock anything over or shove any band memorabilia in his mouth. "Ruby wanted to see you."

"For what, I can't imagine," Crimson said. He crossed his arms as if protecting his precious suit from the emo-band cooties in my room.

I snorted. "Nice to see you, too, bro."

Crimson flashed me a lopsided grin. We butted heads a lot when we were younger, like on that infamous day ten years ago, but we were cool now. When my brother found his fated mate, it really chilled him out. Taylor balanced out his arrogant attitude and brought him down to earth. Honestly, it was nice to see them together. They were a cute couple. Not that I'd admit that out loud.

"We missed you at the beach earlier," Taylor remarked. "We planned a family lunch, remember?"

I blinked. "Huh? Oh, sorry. I didn't remember it was today."

"Were you particularly busy?" Crimson asked, raising a brow. "It looked like you were lazing around in bed."

"I wasn't *lazing*. I was... thinking," I mumbled.

I didn't expect Crimson to remember the significance of the date. He wasn't that interested in my favorite band, the same way I didn't care about his suits. But he knew it was part of my hoard. That was the one thread that connected all dragons. No matter how different we were, dragons intimately understood that bond to a hoard.

"It's TalonStorm," I said quietly. "Today is the ten-year anniversary of their breakup."

Crimson's expression softened. "I see."

"TalonStorm?" Taylor asked.

"My favorite band." I cast a glance at Aquila's poster behind me. "He was the lead singer."

Crimson nodded to the poster. "Thystle was obsessed with him," he murmured to his mate.

"I still am," I corrected.

"I'm sorry to hear that," Taylor said with a sympathetic frown. "Did the members go on to start personal projects or anything?"

I rubbed my arm, feeling cold and empty. "No. They all just... vanished."

The sudden quiet in the room was interrupted as Ruby waddled up to me. He leapt onto my bed, shifted into his dragon form, and gnawed on my pre-ripped jeans. I grinned and patted him on the head.

"Thanks, Ruby," I said. "You're making them even more fashionable."

Ruby squeaked happily. I suddenly felt bad for missing the family lunch earlier. If I'd gone, I would've enjoyed a sunny outing with Ruby, Taylor, and my brothers. Instead, I locked myself in my room, moping over a band that would never return.

Why couldn't I stop thinking about Aquila and Talon-Storm? Anyone else would've forgotten about them by now, or at least accepted the reality that they'd moved on. But I hadn't. I was stuck in the past, pining over an omega who didn't even know I existed.

My mood threatened to spiral again, but my family's presence grounded me. I took a breath and moved past it.

"Sorry I couldn't make it," I said. "I'll remember next time."

To my surprise, Crimson put a hand on my shoulder. "It's all right, Thystle. Sorry you weren't feeling up for it."

I blinked. I wasn't used to him being this affectionate. Taylor really had a positive effect on him.

I was happy for him, but also a bit jealous. How different would my life be if I had a fated mate, too? If Aquila was in it?

"You know what? There's still some leftover hot dogs," Taylor noted. "Why don't you come down to the beach with us? We can have a post-lunch lunch."

I grinned, happy to be included. "That sounds great."

The four of us headed to the beach. Everyone else had scattered to go about their day, but that was fine with me. I was still in a fragile mood, so it was nice not to be over-whelmed by my whole family's presence.

But as soon as I grabbed a lukewarm hot dog and lounged in a beach chair, a flurry of feathers flapped above my head. That could only be one man. A familiar gryphon touched down on the sand, then shifted into his human form, complete with a gaudy fuchsia Hawaiian shirt.

"Good afternoon, drakes and felines!" Gaius said brightly. He took a spare hot dog from the grill without asking. "How are we feeling on this beautiful Wednesday?"

"You know, the Dragonfate Games ended months ago. You can stop talking in that official announcer voice," Crimson said.

Gaius took an offended bite of food. "I'm not doing a voice. This is simply how I speak!"

"Holy Drake, it's worse than I thought," Crimson mumbled. "He doesn't even realize he's doing it..."

Taylor snorted in amusement while Gaius and Crimson engaged in friendly bickering. I ignored them and took another bite of food. I'd been so mired in my feelings, I didn't realize how hungry I'd been.

Gaius interrupted his argument with Crimson to loudly clear his throat. "You sidetracked me, foul dragon. I'm here on a very important mission." He put a finger in the air, summoning everyone's attention. "I bring news from the next island over!"

The unnamed island where Gaius lived was a few dozen miles away, out of sight from the shores of Chromatimaeus Island. Aside from the hotel where our secretary and housekeepers lived permanently, most of the staff who worked on the Dragonfate Games lived on the neighboring island. That meant Gaius's information was probably from them.

Nine months had passed since the first Dragonfate Games. Dragon gestations were unusually short among shifters and Ruby hatched seven months ago, so I wondered if the producers were impatient to shoot the second season. It made sense to film it as soon as possible so they had plenty of time to edit and advertise it.

I'd never watched the first season. Reality TV wasn't my cup of tea, and the idea of binge-watching hours of it bored me to tears. Besides, I'd seen Crimson fall in love in real life. That was enough for me.

"Well? Did the show finally get cancelled?" Crimson asked.

Gaius wagged his finger. "Just the opposite, my friend. Ratings are through the roof. Everyone is clamoring for season two. All our social media pages are flooded with people begging for more!"

Crimson shuddered at the thought. He put an arm around Taylor's waist. "I am *so* glad I got that over with," he mumbled. "It was a blessing in disguise that you all forced me to go first."

I tossed the last piece of bun in my mouth. This conversation had nothing to do with me, so I sank back in the beach chair and relaxed, though I hid under the umbrella so my pale skin didn't get burned by the sun.

"As the host of the show, I'm pivotal to the Dragonfate Games, so Duke and the other producers invited me to a work meeting," Gaius went on, sounding proud of himself. "This morning, we finally decided who the next bachelor should be."

Crimson raised his brows. "Oh? Do tell."

"Drum roll, please..." With a dramatic flourish, Gaius gestured at me. "Our lucky bachelor is Thystle!"

I thought he was joking. When he kept pointing at me, I realized he wasn't.

"You can't be serious," I said.

"I absolutely am!" Gaius confirmed.

Crimson and Taylor turned to look at me. I grew flustered under their gaze. Hell, if I couldn't handle two family members staring at me, how could I handle a TV audience?

I shook my head. "I can't."

"Sure you can," Gaius assured me. "Crimson did it. So can you!"

"No, I can't. I'm not in a good mental state right now," I sputtered. "Why don't you pick Aurum, or Jade, or literally anyone else?"

"We picked you," Gaius stated with finality, flashing me

his award-winning grin. I swore he always used that to his advantage. He should've been a used car salesman.

"It's not so bad," Crimson said wryly. "And you'll do well to remember how pushy all of *you* were when it was my turn in the spotlight."

"It's different when it's someone else," I grumbled.

Taylor came over to give me a sympathetic pat on the back. "Hey, I get it. I don't like that kind of attention either. But honestly, after the first day, you get used to it. And who knows? You could find your fated mate, like Crimson did."

"I won't," I muttered.

"Why do you think that?"

I buried my face in my knees. "Because Aquila is my fated mate, and nobody's seen him for a decade." After a moment, Taylor asked, "What if he's a contestant on the Games?"

My mouth opened to shoot down his idea. It was ridiculous. Yet as I mulled it over, I realized how badly I wanted it to be real. A bud of hope unfurled in my chest.

Slowly, I lifted my head. "What if he *was* a contestant?" I suggested.

Gaius swooped in to encourage me. "And why can't he be? It's like I said, Thystle. The ratings for this show are wild! Humans, shifters, it doesn't matter. We're anticipating a huge surge in applicants for season two. We'll reach out to his agent! It would be a great opportunity for him."

"Aquila's been AWOL for a decade. I don't know if he even has an agent to reach out to," I murmured.

But that didn't stop the hopeful pitter-patter of my heart. If Aquila was on the show, I'd finally get my chance to be with him, like we were always meant to be. But to entice him, we'd have to get the word out. The Dragonfate Games had to be an attractive option.

I leapt out of my chair. "Gaius. Get Duke and the producers to go all out on advertising. Spread the application to as many omegas as possible. I want the island full of them."

Crimson gawked. "You cannot be serious."

"I'm dead serious, Crimson," I stated, glaring at him.

Gaius didn't share his friend's distaste for crowds. He grinned, pleased at my sudden mood flip. "Yes, sir!"

Crimson was still stuck on my comment. "Why the change of heart?"

"This could be my chance to bring Aquila out of hiding," I said.

Crimson sighed like I was being ridiculous and shook his head. "Thystle, I know you're obsessed with Aquila, but be realistic. If nobody's seen the guy in a decade, what makes you think he'll apply to be on the Games?"

I bristled at my brother's negativity. "He *has* to."

"He doesn't have to do anything," Crimson pointed out. "Why don't you focus on the omegas who already *want* to be here? Don't box yourself in. Who knows? You may fall in love with someone right in front of you."

I frowned but didn't argue with him. There was no point. Crimson never understood my love for Aquila, and he wasn't about to start now.

Gaius, on the other hand, was thrilled at my enthusiasm. "Then it's settled! Omegas galore! Omegas everywhere, taking over the island!"

Taylor raised a brow. "Maybe you shouldn't phrase it that way."

"Willing applicants thirsting for love!" Gaius corrected without missing a beat. His enthusiasm wasn't quelled by anything. "I'll go tell the producers. Ooh, this is so exciting! Our little Thystle's growing up."

"Why am I little? I'm a grown man," I grumbled.

Gaius had already shifted and took wing. I felt hopeful knowing he'd do everything in his power to grant my wish. The bigger the pool of applicants, the better chance Aquila would be among them...

Right?

THREE

Matteo
_____

WHY WAS it so hard to find a decent plain white shirt in this city?

I sighed as I put the hanger back on the rack. The shirt I picked up looked promising before I noticed the tiny embroidered logo on the pocket. I didn't want a logo, or a graphic, or even fancy stitching. I wanted an unobtrusive, simple white button-up. I wanted to blend into the background.

To be invisible.

That was my plan on the first season of the Dragon-fate Games—and it worked. I was ordinary. I dressed simply. I acted polite, but not overly so. I didn't want to broadcast anything special about myself. My reward was that nobody talked about my appearance on the show. I was never the topic of discussion on social media threads. I only lurked in those places, since I didn't have any accounts. The fewer channels for people to contact me through, the better.

I was happy about that. Nothing good ever came of fame. Not for me, anyway.

I flipped through the hangers until I landed on the

perfect shirt. White. Long-sleeved. As dull as watching paint dry.

Perfect.

I bought it in my size and left the store. That was the last item of clothing I needed for my trip. The rest I'd bring from my closet at home.

Any day now, I expected a call from Winnie, the secretary from Chromatimaeus Island. After the Dragonfate Games' first season was over, the producers offered me a return ticket for season two. It was my choice whether or not to accept, but in the end, I took it without hesitation.

The first alpha dragon bachelor, Crimson, wasn't my fated mate. I knew that the moment I met him. Unlike other contestants, like that cat shifter, Alaric, I never tried to force love. It would come for me when it did. I was happy for my friend Taylor rightfully winning the season—and Crimson's love.

But Crimson wasn't the only alpha dragon on the island. That's what brought me back. Deep down, I sensed my fated mate was there. Otherwise, I'd never risk appearing on TV again.

Thankfully, my plain persona didn't attract much attention, and I planned to keep it that way.

With my brown bag clutched in hand, I headed down the street towards my apartment. Or, I tried to. The sidewalk was blocked by a huge crowd of excited, rowdy people.

I would've crossed the street to escape them, but I'd have to jaywalk through four lanes of traffic. Too bad I lived in a human-dominant city. If I didn't, I could've simply shifted into my golden eagle form and flown.

I braced myself for the crowd and skirted the edge of it. Something had them all riled up. I didn't care to learn what it was—until I heard a familiar phrase.

"...so apply now to the Dragonfate Games! Who knows? The next winner could be *you*!"

I stopped in my tracks.

That voice...

Curiosity got the best of me and I peered into the crowd. They all gathered around a storefront's glass window where huge high-definition TVs played familiar picturesque footage from Chromatimaeus Island.

But at the center of attention was an even more familiar sight—Gaius in the flesh, wearing one of his typical Hawaiian shirts. This time it was an eye-searing shade of cyan.

I nearly dropped my bag. What was he doing here?

Gaius didn't notice me. He went on in his charismatic announcer voice, grabbing everyone's attention. "All omega shifters between the ages of twenty-five and fifty are eligible to apply!"

That was odd. I didn't recall there being a strict age range like that on the first application. I wondered about the reasoning behind it.

"So, what are you waiting for?" Gaius preached. "Who doesn't want a chance to be an alpha dragon's fated mate? Simply fill out the form and you're golden!"

Swayed by Gaius's pitch, everyone clamored to reach the table with the forms. I stood back so I didn't get run over. There was a civil line when I first applied, nothing nearly as wild as this. Did people want to be fated mates with a dragon this badly?

Though, I supposed I wasn't any different. I knew deep in my heart my fated mate was on that island. Who was to say these people applying didn't feel the same way?

I side-stepped the commotion to speak to Gaius privately. When he saw me, his face lit up.

"Matteo!" He gave me a friendly hug. "Good to see

you, my fellow feathered friend! What a coincidence. Didn't imagine I'd run into a previous contestant today."

"Same here. I can't believe this crowd, either. Were the Games really that popular?"

"Can eagles fly?" He grinned. "And season two is going to be much bigger—bachelor's orders."

My brows rose, and my heart fluttered softly. "Oh? Who is it this time, if I may ask?"

"Sure, it's no secret. He wants the whole world to know."

Gaius pressed a button on his remote and gestured to the flat screen TV. The scene changed. The beautiful shots of the beach disappeared, and in their place was a model-worthy still of Thystle. His long, wispy purple hair flowed against the pillow he lay on, and his half-lidded eyes graced with black eyeliner gave the camera a confident, sultry look.

My heart skipped a beat. I'd only seen Thystle once in person during season one's closing ceremony, but even then, he'd struck me as special. All of the dragon brothers were gorgeous, obviously, but there was a magnetic quality about the young alpha with the black-rimmed amethyst gaze.

A shudder went down my spine as I locked eyes with the Thystle on the screen. And apparently, I wasn't the only one interested in him. Once Gaius flipped the switch, the crowd was drawn to him. They gathered around the TV, still clutching their application forms. Now that they'd actually seen the grand prize, they were even more eager to enter.

I found myself grinding my teeth, which I usually never did. I stopped.

It didn't matter if all these people entered—or were even accepted. I'd already been offered a return ticket, so

I had a guaranteed spot in the second season of the Games.

But if Thystle actually chose me... that was a different story.

There was no use worrying about it now. Besides, I'd never even spoken to the man. I couldn't fantasize about being his fated mate without at least sharing a conversation.

"Thanks for chatting, Gaius," I said. "I'd better be on my way."

He nodded at my brown bag.

"More shopping?" He peered into the bag and looked disappointed. "Oh... A plain white shirt? Nothing more colorful?"

"Not everyone is as flamboyant as you," I said, arching a brow playfully.

He grinned and puffed out his chest, clearly taking pride in it. "True. If everybody was, I wouldn't stand out nearly as much."

After saying goodbye, I went on my way. I was happy to be away from the crowd. I hoped there wouldn't be *that* many contestants on season two. If there were, how would Thystle ever choose a winner?

But my concerns quickly floated away. That wasn't how fated mates worked. One would always pick their fated mate out of a crowd, no matter how many people there were.

That's what I thought, anyway. Not like I had a fated mate to test my theory.

As I made my way down the sidewalk, I passed a store with an open door blasting a news stream. The high volume was so jarring that I turned to frown in the store's direction. It was a pop-culture place selling the latest fad items.

I was about to walk away and forget all about it until I heard something that stopped me dead in my tracks.

"...former members of TalonStorm announced their return!"

The breath escaped my lungs. I felt like a truck had hit me. I stared wide-eyed at the open door where the news broadcast came from. A handful of employees flocked around the laptop playing the stream, excitedly talking over it.

Did I really just hear that? I thought, unsure of myself.

I paused, ready to write it off as a hallucination, but the announcer kept going.

"This is not a drill, people. Our breaking intel has it that two of the three former members, Vani and Keaux, are debuting a brand-new—"

I couldn't listen anymore.

Desperate to get out of earshot of the blaring voice, I bolted down the sidewalk. Chills ran down my arms, and my chest felt coated in tar.

Vani and Keaux.

Those were names I'd tried not to think about for the past decade. Names I'd tried to escape from.

Why? Why were they coming up again now?

My mind was a blur until I reached the lobby of my apartment building. I'd worked up a cold sweat despite the heat. Just as I went to wipe it away, my phone rang. I got ready to swipe reject until I saw the caller ID was from Chromatimaeus Island.

"Hello?"

"Hi, Matteo!" Winnie said excitedly. "How are you today?"

I didn't want to worry her, so I lied. "I'm good. What's up?"

"I'm calling to tell you to pack your bags—your flight back to the island is in two weeks!"

That was so soon, but at the same time, didn't feel soon enough. I wished I could teleport back to that pristine white beach right now.

"I'll be there," I promised.

"I've also gone ahead and booked the same hotel room for you. Just to make things easier since the rooms are getting pretty full."

That didn't sound promising. "A lot more contestants?"

"Yup." She sighed. "Gaius keeps sending me more and more applications. It's taken me all day to sort them... I don't know why Thystle wanted so many omegas on season two."

"*He* wanted more applicants?" I asked, surprised.

"Right? I was shocked, too. It seems so unlike him... Anyway, I've forwarded you the ticket info. See you soon, and good luck!"

After I hung up, I stood aimlessly in the lobby. I couldn't stop thinking about my next trip to the island. It was a welcome reprieve from the gnawing anxiety I'd felt earlier.

I took a deep breath. No need for my feathers to get ruffled. I wasn't in any danger, and in a week, I'd be on an all-expenses paid vacation on a private island.

Except it wasn't really a vacation, was it? I'd be fighting talon and wing, competing against other omegas in the Dragonfate Games. And apparently, there were a *lot* more of them this time around.

I may have been a plain golden eagle, but I was no pushover. If Thystle was my true mate, I'd do anything to win.

I just had to trust fate.

FOUR

Thystle

AS I WATCHED the director shout orders at the staff, I turned the volume up on my CD player. Duke was so damned loud. How did such a short creature have a voice that could level a building?

The rest of the filming staff ran around like worker ants, dutifully taking care of everything. Producing a TV show took a ton of work and money. I wondered if my brother, Saffron, considered that when he originally pitched the idea. I was glad I didn't have to do anything except *be* on the show.

I sat nestled into a shaded chair on the edge of the beach, clutching my CD player. Duke ordered me to sit nearby in case he needed my input, but he barely asked me anything. I think he just wanted to waste my time. The only work I'd done for the show was to take a "sexy" modelling photo as advertising for the Games.

I shut my eyes and sighed. This was all such a pain... Why couldn't Aquila manifest right in front of me? All my problems would instantly be solved.

Someone tapped the bridge of my headphones. A

burst of anger erupted through my body. My human teeth shifted into dragon fangs as I whirled around.

"What?" I snapped.

"Geez, don't bite my fingers off," Aurum said, shrinking away.

I glared at him. My fangs slowly changed back. "You know I hate it when people do that."

"Sorry." Aurum shrugged. "Your eyes were closed, so it wasn't like I could dance around in front of you to get your attention."

"What do you want?" I asked.

Crimson strolled up beside Aurum with an amused smirk. I got the feeling he'd used Aurum as a meat shield in case I *did* bite someone's fingers off.

"I'm here to give you a friendly pep talk," Crimson said. "I'm not sure why Aurum tagged along."

Aurum plopped down in the sand next to my chair. "Bored."

"So you came to bother me?" I grumbled.

Crimson cleared his throat. "Anyway. Thystle, you've invited quite a few omegas to the Games this time around. Are you sure you can keep up with them all?"

I bristled. "What's that supposed to mean?"

"Like, are you gonna remember everyone's name?" Aurum chimed in. "People get annoyed if you forget their names."

"I don't *have* to remember everyone's name," I argued. "It's not like I'm going to address every single one of them. Only one of them is important."

Aurum snorted. "Make sure Duke gets that statement on film. Then you'll be really popular!"

"Shut up."

Crimson sighed. "Thystle, I get where you're coming from. When the Games started, I took interest in Taylor immediately. I *knew* he was the one. But you still have be civil with the other contestants."

"Why are you guys treating me like I'm some dickhead? Are you confusing me with Viol, the *actual* asshole purple dragon in our family?" I grumbled.

"I'm saying how you treat them matters. If you write off every omega because he's not Aquila, you might end up alone."

I wrinkled my nose at him. "You wrote off every omega who wasn't Taylor, so I dunno why you think you're qualified to lecture me."

Crimson crossed his arms. "I mean, yes, I did, but—"

I went to put my headphones back on.

"Wait, Thystle," Aurum interrupted. "You're not even interested in *any* of the hotties from season one?"

"I didn't watch it," I admitted.

He sputtered. "You didn't?"

Crimson's jaw dropped. "You didn't even watch the show your brother starred in... I'm offended."

I rolled my eyes at their melodrama. "Guys, it's not the type of show I'm interested in, okay? And what's the point? I'm gonna be *on* the show, so why would I need to watch it?"

Aurum frowned. "Well, if you haven't seen it, how'd you know your beloved Aquila hasn't already been on it?"

I paused. I never watched the show, but I saw the contestants during the closing ceremony. Truth be told, I hadn't paid close attention to their faces, and even if I had, it wouldn't have mattered. The Aquila I knew and loved always wore a costume mask that covered his entire face except for his eyes. Besides, what the hell were the odds that *my* fated mate was a rejected omega on Crimson's season of the Games? In any case, I was sick of my brothers interrogating me.

"He wasn't there," I stated, then reached for my headphones again.

Aurum snatched them from me. "Dude, are you serious? You are so stubborn sometimes."

"Give me that!" I snarled.

As we wrestled for the headphones, Crimson sighed behind us. "I should've known my advice was pointless."

I won the war. After reclaiming my precious headphones, I glared daggers at Aurum. He stood up and dusted the sand off his pants with a sour expression.

"You know, just for that, I hope Aquila *isn't* on season two," Aurum spat.

My eyes widened. "Take that back. *Take it back right now.*"

"No."

Rage fueled me. Throwing the headphones down, I leapt at my brother. We clawed at each other with our dragon talons out, both spitting with anger.

"Oh, for Holy Drake's sake," Crimson complained loudly. "Did we hire security on set?"

From the corner of my eye, I saw a big flash of yellow. Suddenly, a force barrelled into my side. I grunted as I landed a few feet away from Aurum. When I got up, I saw Saffron's dragon form arched in front of Aurum, protecting him. My own brother bared his fangs at me.

When it was obvious the fight was over, the spikes along Saffron's spine lowered.

"Are you okay?" he asked his twin.

"Yeah, I'm fine," Aurum said, shaking the sand off his clothes.

I frowned. Saffron didn't ask *me* if I was okay.

A mix of anger and sadness welled up inside of me. Brotherly love was different than romantic love, but it was love all the same. And I didn't feel that from anybody.

Feeling crabby and alone, I grabbed my CD player and stalked off. The staff were too busy to notice I'd left, and none of my brothers followed me. That filled me with smug defiance that I was right after all, but it also made me feel like crap.

I walked along the edge of the shore, glad to be away from the noise and commotion. The sound of the gentle waves relaxed me. Sort of. I couldn't stop thinking about Aquila, and how nervous I was for his appearance on the show.

But doubt wormed its way through my brain. What if, after all the work I'd done, he didn't enter the Games? Was I stupid for thinking he'd be here?

I sighed and sat on the ledge of a boulder, looking out at the ocean. I put my headphones on and hit play.

TalonStorm's debut album, *Wings of the Sun*—my favorite album of all time—began playing. Vani and Keaux were on electric guitar and drums, respectively. But Aquila's voice rose above it all. That beautiful, melodic, raw voice that gutted me every single time. It was the voice I heard in my dreams. The one I so desperately wanted to hear in real life, whispering in my ear and telling me everything would be all right...

I got too emotional, so I ripped the headphones off and wiped the tears from my eyes. Even though I was alone, I couldn't look weak. Now that filming was nearly underway, I never knew when a kobold would be hiding in the bushes, filming me when I least expected it.

I was an alpha dragon, a creature meant to be strong and confident. But how could I be when I felt like I was missing my other half?

A deep voice came out of nowhere. "Don't discard them. Your tears are one more drop for the ocean."

Cobalt's sudden appearance scared the crap out of me. I turned around to see him standing on the boulder.

"It would be nice if everyone stopped manifesting behind me today," I mumbled.

Cobalt ignored my tongue-in-cheek comment and sat next to me. With his tall stature and broad shoulders, he seemed as big as the boulder itself.

"It's always okay to cry," he said, "but if you'd like to talk it out, we can."

I rubbed my arm, feeling embarrassed. Cobalt was so cool and calm all the time. Meanwhile, I was the most emotional out of everyone. The emo label wasn't for nothing.

"I'm just... lonely," I said under my breath.

Cobalt nodded stoically. He said nothing, giving me space to continue.

"And nobody understands how I feel about Aquila," I went on. "They think it's some kind of stupid obsession, like my feelings about him aren't real."

Cobalt faced me. "I don't think that, Thystle. Your feelings *are* real." He pulled up his sleeve and held up his bare forearm. "You proved that to me ten years ago."

Emotion welled up in my chest. Cobalt's challenge meant a lot to me. Despite the thin line of scars that remained, the wounds had healed well, but I still remembered the day I sank my fangs into him to prove myself. If nobody else did, at least he believed in my obsessive faith.

I blew out a breath, feeling a bit better. "Thanks, Cobalt."

He nodded. "I hope you meet your fated mate soon. I want that for you. For all of us."

My heart fluttered as I thought about Aquila.

"Yeah," I said wistfully. "Me, too."

FIVE

Matteo
─────────

I FELT like a sardine packed in a tin, but at least the hotel was still nice.

The plane landed earlier that day, unloading a metric ton of ecstatic omegas who swarmed the hotel. Winnie wasn't joking about the rooms filling up. Not a single empty one remained. Everywhere I looked, there was a fresh face—competition in finding my fated mate.

I forced myself not to get caught up in the hype. Fated mates *always* found each other, no matter the circumstances. It didn't matter if there was one other omega here, or a hundred. If Thystle and I were meant for each other, it would all work out in the end.

But that didn't stop me from getting annoyed at a solid chunk of the other contestants for existing, especially when they clogged up the damn hallways like a bunch of frat boys in their first year of college.

The producers didn't waste any time. Filming had already begun. Kobold crew members casually followed us around, giving us time to get accustomed to the cameras. I was used to them already, but some of the new guys were *interested* in them, to say the least. They put on pompous airs, acting like each camera was their own personal YouTube audience.

I kept my distance from those people.

We had the day to relax and prepare for the meet-and-greet that evening. There was an ice breaker for the contestants in the hotel lobby, which I attended despite being wary of the crowd. There must've been at least three dozen contestants. I searched for anyone I recognized. I couldn't be the only omega from season one who'd accepted the invitation to return, could I?

As I scanned the lobby, I heard a shrill yowl behind me. I turned to see a tall omega I didn't recognize, and a shorter one that I did—Alaric, the Angora cat shifter from season one.

Alaric's face twisted in an offended snarl. The other omega awkwardly held an empty cup.

"Watch where you're going," Alaric snapped. "You spilled your ice-cold water all over my shoes."

The other guy shrugged, already turning to leave. "Geez, sorry, pal."

Alaric scoffed. "That's all you have to say? What about a genuine apology?"

But it was no use. The water-dumping perpetrator disappeared into the undulating crowd.

I strode towards Alaric before he blew his fuse, which I knew he was fully capable of doing. I'd witnessed plenty of his bratty antics on season one. Yet compared to the rowdy unknown of the new omegas, Alaric's sourpuss attitude almost felt comforting.

"Hey. It's good to see a familiar face," I said.

Alaric's scowl faded when he recognized me. "Oh, it's you. You're that peregrine falcon shifter, right?"

"Golden eagle," I corrected, although I wasn't bothered by his error. The fact that he barely remembered me was a good thing. If I didn't stand out to a fellow contestant, I wouldn't to a worldwide audience, either.

"Yes, right," Alaric murmured. "So, you returned for another chance at a dragon mate?"

"Same as you," I pointed out.

He sighed, crossing his arms. "You're not wrong about that..."

"Have you seen anyone else from season one?"

He huffed. "I can't see much of anything over this writhing mass of bodies. Whose bright idea was it to invite all these people?"

"Thystle's, apparently."

Alaric paused, then cleared his throat. "I see. From what I know of him, I didn't think he was the party boy type."

"What *do* you know of him?" I asked.

I'd assumed Alaric had the same amount of knowledge as me, but I wouldn't put it past him to do some pre-show digging about the bachelor. On season one, he was hell-bent on winning and becoming the dragon's mate... but obviously Crimson's heart lay solely with Taylor. It didn't surprise me that Alaric's determination—or was it desperation?—carried over to season two.

Alaric leaned closer to me and lowered his voice, wanting to keep it between us. "Rumor has it he's obsessed with emo bands."

I didn't judge books by their covers, but Thystle's appearance definitely gave off that vibe. If that was true, then we shared that interest. Despite our turbulent relationship, music was my secret love. But I wasn't about to tell Alaric about it. I didn't want anybody to know the truth—not even Thystle.

"I texted Taylor to ask, and he confirmed that Thystle

hoards music, specifically of that genre. And then he sent a picture of his baby. Ugh, he was so cute."

Alaric's face screwed up in thought. "But isn't that strange? Don't emo people sit in their rooms and mope alone? Why would he invite an entire college dorm full of omegas?"

I shrugged. "Your interests don't define your preferences. Maybe he's more social than you thought."

Alaric didn't look convinced. "We'll see, I suppose," he mumbled, then nodded his head. "Hey, isn't that the annoying dog from last time?"

I turned just in time to see another familiar face pop up among the sea of people. It was Muzo, the black-backed jackal shifter. His head popped up, then sank back down and disappeared, over and over again. He looked like popcorn in the microwave.

"I think he's trying to reach us," I commented.

Alaric snorted. "Good luck to him getting past those goons."

"Matteo!" Muzo called between grunts as he pogo-sticked up and down. "Alaric! Yoohoo!"

As I turned to help him get through, one of the big omegas in his way suddenly snarled. "Hey, asshole! You stepped on my foot!"

Muzo yelped. "Oops, sorry! Just trying to get through—"

The man bared his teeth in Muzo's face. "By bouncing around like an idiot?"

I'd seen enough fights break out in my life to know where this was going. Acting fast, I rushed towards them. Muzo wasn't the brawling type, but he had the kind of whimsically clueless personality that pissed off hotheads looking to throw the first punch.

"Sorry, man," Muzo said. "You're so tall that I can't see past you."

As I got closer, I saw snow-white hair and heard a softer voice behind him. They belonged to Poppy, the arctic wolf shifter from season one.

Poppy's voice trembled, just like the rest of him. "Muzo, don't argue, let's just go..."

"I'm not arguing!" Muzo argued. "I'm just tellin' the truth. This guy's huge, so he's blocking my line of sight."

The omega roared. "You calling me huge, pipsqueak?"

Muzo's eyes widened as he realized the danger he was in. "W-wait, not like that!" he yelped.

Too late. The big omega drew back his arm—with a large, tight fist at the end of it.

My heart lurched. Muzo was so small that the force of the blow would knock his teeth out, if it didn't knock *him* out first.

Acting fast, I threw myself between them.

The man's fist caught the side of my head. Pain shot out from my temple, dizzying me for a second. I stood my ground and tried to keep my legs steady.

Poppy gasped in fear behind me.

"Matteo!" Muzo cried out.

I saw stars and couldn't speak, but I held up a hand to let them know I was okay.

"Dude, what the hell?" the man shouted. An angry vein popped in his forehead. "Why'd you get in my way?" His breath stank of booze, but it wasn't being served in the lobby. The jerk must've snuck his own onto the island.

I shook off the addled sensation with a low groan. "Ever heard the saying, 'pick on somebody your own size'?" I asked.

Shockingly, that didn't calm his fury. He snarled at me. "Oh, like *you?*"

"No, I—"

My sentence was cut short as the man took another swing at me. This time I got clobbered on the opposite side of my face.

By now, everyone around us had noticed the fight. A few fellow jerks actually cheered—I suspected *they* were boozed up, too—but most people shouted angrily at the perpetrator.

I swayed on my feet, then felt a pair of hands grabbing my arms to keep me upright. Poppy and Muzo had my back.

"Are you crazy?" Muzo demanded.

"Leave him alone!" Poppy said. His gentle voice was louder than I'd ever heard it, yet barely audible over the crowd. Still, it warmed my heart that he tried to protect me.

"It's fine, you two," I mumbled, but it came out less confident than I intended.

A sharp, ear-splitting whistle rang out. The crowd dispersed as two stocky, stoic-faced kobolds burst through. Their short stature didn't stop them from looking intimidating.

"Violence is strictly forbidden," one barked at the fist-swinging omega.

"And bringing your own booze, too," the other boomed, holding a flask. They must've ferreted it out of his room. If he was as smart as his behavior indicated, I doubted he'd done a good job of hiding it.

"You're out!"

The kobold security crew escorted the perpetrator back to his room. Once he was gone, a kobold medic rushed towards me.

Good timing, too—just before she reached me, I swayed and passed out.

SIX

Thystle

_____

"A *FIGHT?*" I choked out. "In the *lobby?*"

I'd been on my way to take a much-needed nap in my room before that evening's meet-and-greet began when Jade stopped me in the hallway to drop the bombshell.

"Yes, I'm afraid so," Jade said with a sigh. Since the first season of the Dragonfate Games, he'd taken on an administrative role between Duke's film crew and us dragons. He was responsible and orderly, with a friendlier demeanor than Cobalt, so it was no surprise he took on the task.

What *was* a surprise was that some dickhead started a fight in the hotel lobby before the Games even began.

I gawked at Jade, unable to believe what he'd said. "Who does something like that?"

"Someone intoxicated, that's who," Jade replied, pushing up the rim of his glasses. "Sometimes, being on reality TV brings out the worst in people..."

"Where'd he even get the alcohol? They only serve it at the meet-and-greet, but it hasn't started yet."

"He brought it with him, against the clearly established rules," Jade said with a tight frown. "Needless to say, he was kicked off the show immediately, along with the others found to possess alcohol."

"There were *more?*"

Jade sighed. "Yes. They've all been put on a plane home and won't be participating in the Games."

"Was anyone hurt?" I asked.

Jade grimaced. "Unfortunately, yes."

Guilt wormed its way through my chest. I wasn't responsible for any person's actions, but it still felt like my fault.

"Who is it?"

"The victim was Matteo, one of the returning contestants from season one."

The name didn't ring a bell, which made me feel even guiltier. The guy got hurt because of me and I didn't even know who he was. The least I could do was apologize in person.

But then another thought struck me. If someone had gotten hurt on set, would the whole show be cancelled? Was that how TV worked? Ugh, I should've paid attention when Duke explained everything to me. If the show was cancelled, I'd lose the possibility of meeting Aquila—*if* he was even here. Surely with the entry requirements and the number of omegas here, there had to be a chance...

"Thystle?" Jade asked when I didn't respond.

I seated myself back in reality. "How badly was he hurt? Can I see him?" I asked.

Jade mulled it over. "I suppose there's no harm in it. He's in the medical ward, here in the castle."

"Wait, why here? Isn't there a nurse's room in the hotel?"

"There was, but the crew repurposed it as a regular room to accommodate the number of contestants. So, no."

I winced. I was starting to think inviting so many

people was a bad idea. First the forbidden alcohol slipping through, then the lobby brawl, now this. But how was I supposed to know they'd behave badly? The omegas on Crimson's season were all so normal. *Too* normal. None of them could've been Aquila, the celebrity superstar.

"I'll go apologize to him," I suggested.

Jade nodded. "That's a good idea. It's good optics for the show."

"No, I don't want cameras filming him when he's down. They probably already got the whole fight on film..." Jade smiled warmly. "True. I'm sure he'll appreciate that."

A pair of footsteps thundered around the corner.

"Did you guys see the fight?" Aurum asked, out of breath. He wore a backwards baseball cap, for some reason. "It was awesome!"

"I feel so bad for that guy," Saffron added, following him, a knit beanie perched on his head. His hat, like Aurum's, covered his hair, making it harder to differentiate them. The only way I could tell them apart right now was that Aurum enjoyed brawls more than Saffron. I guessed Saffron had taken the lion's share of the empathy in their shared egg.

I bristled at the twins' sudden appearance. I was still pissed at Aurum because of our tiff earlier, and to a lesser extent, Saffron for defending him, which he always did.

"A man got hurt, if you even give a shit," I grumbled at Aurum. "And why are you wearing those stupid hats?"

"Hey, I care! I just said I feel bad for him," Saffron argued.

"Besides, he wasn't seriously hurt," Aurum pointed out. "He's awake right now."

"How do you know that?" I demanded.

Aurum shrugged, spinning his baseball hat around. "'Cause we went to see him."

I didn't know why, but a rush of jealousy filled my blood. I was the bachelor this season, and Matteo's injury was my fault. It was my responsibility to deal with Matteo, not theirs. I hated that they went to visit him before I got the chance.

"Why *are* you wearing those hats?" Jade asked curiously.

Aurum grinned like a kid who felt no guilt about breaking the rules. "Last year was boring. We wanted to see the contestants up close. So we went to mingle." He pointed to the hat. "With disguises, of course."

I rolled my eyes. The twins had only appeared in human form during last season's closing ceremony for about five minutes. I doubted any of the new contestants remembered them. They just wanted an excuse to wear those stupid hats.

"Yeah, nobody looked twice at us, except one hot dude who asked a lot of questions about you," Saffron agreed.

I ignored the comment about the hot dude. All I could think about was poor Matteo's injury.

Saffron waved his hand. "There were so many people that we got lost in the crowd, anyway. It was stuffy in that lobby with all those bodies, and not in a sexy way."

Another pang of guilt hit me. The show hadn't even started, and I'd already caused a big mess.

I stormed past the twins, impatient to reach the medical ward. A kobold nurse sat on a stool by the door. It was slightly ajar.

She pointedly raised a brow at me. "Are you here to cause trouble like those other dragons?" she asked in a stern tone.

I cursed the twins.

"No, I'm here to apologize to Matteo," I said.

She nodded for me to go inside. Ignoring the random anxious feeling in my chest, I opened the door.

The room was spacious and clean. A man lay in a bed by an open window, letting in the fresh ocean breeze.

My heart sank when he turned towards me.

He had not one but two black eyes.

Oh, Holy Drake, I'm the worst bachelor of a dating show ever, I thought miserably.

"Hey," Matteo said. His voice was cool and casual. That was a good sign. At least he wasn't instantly berating me.

"Hi," I replied. "Is it okay if I come in?"

A smile curled the edge of his mouth. "This is your home, isn't it? You don't need my permission."

"Yeah, but *you're* the one injured in bed," I countered.

"True. I'd like the company, in any case. Grab a chair."

I sat on a stool next to him. He looked awful. The flesh around both his eyes was swollen and purple, making it difficult to see his brown eyes clearly. It was a shame, because otherwise, he was robustly handsome.

As I regarded his face, I tried to recall him from the season one contestants... and fell flat. Why didn't I remember him?

Matteo chuckled. "You look like a sad puppy right now."

"Huh?"

"You seem guilty, like you committed a heinous crime."

"I *am* guilty! It's my fault you got hurt. I feel terrible."

"With all due respect, I have two black eyes," Matteo said with a dry grin. "I think *I'm* the one who feels terrible."

I groaned. "Yeah, you're right."

"I'm joking, Thystle."

My heart fluttered when he said my name. He already knew it, but the only reason I knew his name was because Jade told me.

"So, what brings you here to my sickbed?" Matteo asked. At least he was in a good mood.

"I came to apologize," I murmured. "I heard about the fight. I'm so sorry, that never should've happened on my watch."

Matteo seemed a bit surprised. "How could you stop a fight you weren't present for?"

"Still. I invited a lot of contestants. Too many, by the sound of it," I mumbled.

Matteo shrugged. "The producers should've known how many contestants the show could accommodate. It's their responsibility to deal with that sort of thing, not yours."

I made a face at him. "Are you always this logical?"

He grinned. "Sorry. I'll let you mope, emo kid."

My eyes widened, rising in my seat. "Wait. What did you just say?"

Matteo's expression flickered with hesitation. "I'm sorry, that was too forward of me—"

"You know the difference!" I cried, ecstatic. "You know I'm emo and not goth!"

Matteo's jaw dropped, then he laughed in relief. "Well, yeah. It's obvious. Doesn't everybody?"

In my excitement, I grabbed his arm. "No! My idiotic brothers call me goth all the time when they're making fun of me!"

Matteo clicked his tongue disapprovingly. "You should keep better company."

"Like you," I said, leaning forward in my seat. I couldn't help myself. I'd never met a single person in real life who understood that part of my identity, and now one had been served to me on a silver platter. Er, hospital bed.

Matteo paused and blinked, which looked painful given his swollen eyes. "If you say so."

At his hesitation, I realized my hand was clamped on his arm. I let go and sat back in my seat with an awkward clear of my throat.

"My bad," I said. "Um, anyway. What was I saying? Oh, right. Sorry about... everything. We got rid of the boozed-up dickheads, so there shouldn't be any more problems."

"That's good," Matteo said, nodding.

"Do you want monetary compensation or something? For the injuries?"

My offer was genuine, but Matteo chuckled like I was being silly. "The nurse cleared me of anything serious, like a concussion. It's only a plain old pair of black eyes. I'll live. But I appreciate it."

I sighed in relief. "What happened anyway? You don't strike me as the type to get into fights."

He grinned. "Good observation. I'm not. I stepped in to protect one of the smaller omegas, Muzo. He got on the wrong side of a 'boozed-up dickhead,' as you so delightfully put it."

When Matteo mentioned the name, a face popped into my head. Muzo was that omega jackal from season one. I remembered his wacky grin among the crowd at the closing ceremony, and how wildly he'd clapped and cheered for his friend Taylor. Hell, I recalled Poppy, Taylor's arctic wolf friend, too. He had a baby face and clapped softly, like he was afraid of making too much noise and bothering somebody.

Matteo was Taylor's friend, too, wasn't he? So why didn't I remember *him?*

"That was really nice of you," I said.

"Anybody would've done the same."

I snorted, thinking about Aurum's willingness to fight me earlier. "No, they wouldn't. Trust me."

Matteo was quiet as he regarded me for a moment. Dammit, I wished I could've seen his eyes better. Past the unfortunate swelling, they looked warm and kind.

"In any case, thanks for coming to talk to me," he said. "You're a busy bachelor, and this has taken time out of your day."

"Don't even mention it. I'm not as busy as you think. Until the show starts, all I do is sit around and look pretty."

He tilted his head. "And you do a fine job of that."

Heat prickled my cheeks. The sudden compliment caught me off guard. It didn't feel forced, or like he was trying to get on my good side before the Games officially began. He really meant it.

"Thanks," I said, running a hand through my hair to distract from my blushing face. I decided to change the subject. "By the way, I apologize for my idiot brothers bothering you earlier. If I'd known about their scheme, I would've told the nurse to lock the door."

Matteo's mouth curled in amusement. "Not at all. They were only here for a minute before she chased them away."

An unexpected laugh came out of me. "She did? They conveniently failed to mention that part."

"It was quite a scene," Matteo agreed. "I've never seen a kobold roar at a pair of dragons like that."

"Wish I'd seen it. Maybe they should come bother you again," I joked.

He arched a handsome brow. "I'd much prefer *you* bother me instead."

The heat in my cheeks had barely settled, but now it flared again.

As I gazed at him and laughed with him, a realization hit me.

I *liked* Matteo.

The Dragonfate Games hadn't even started yet, and here I was falling for the first omega I spoke to. Was that normal? Did this happen to Crimson with Taylor?

I tried to quiet the fluttering sensation in my chest. "The meet-and-greet is in an hour, so I'll have plenty of chances to bother you more."

He flashed me a radiant smile. "Then I hope the nurse clears me in time."

"What?"

"If she says I'm too injured to participate, I'll have to stay here."

My stomach flipped. I hadn't considered the possibility that Matteo would miss it because of his injuries.

"Then I won't go," I stated flat-out.

Surprise crossed Matteo's face. "Why?"

I shrugged and got comfortable in my seat. "There's no point if you're not there. I'll hang out here with you instead."

For a few beats, Matteo was silent with astonishment. "Thystle, you can't do that."

I smirked. "I'm the alpha dragon bachelor. I can do whatever I like. And if I want to spend all evening in the medical ward with you, nobody can stop me."

A rosy hue colored Matteo's face—and it wasn't from the inflammation.

He parted his mouth. "Thystle—"

The door burst open. An obnoxiously dressed Gaius flounced into the room. For a second, I saw the kobold nurse behind him. She looked smitten. I guessed Gaius had sweet-talked his way in.

Unlike her, I wasn't as pleased to see him.

"What are you doing here?" I asked, grumpy that my alone time with Matteo had been interrupted.

Unlike my stupid brothers, Gaius was more perceptive than he let on. With a single glance, he understood what had transpired here.

"Hello, Matteo! Sorry to hear about the incident. And I'm even sorrier to whisk you away like this, Thystle," Gaius said, shooting both of us a sympathetic look, "but Duke *screamed* at me to fetch you for the meet-and-greet. His voice is still ringing in my ears..."

"If Matteo's not going, then I'm not, either," I griped.

Gaius stroked his chin. "Hm, that is a pickle, isn't it? What do you say, nurse? Can you clear our buddy for an easygoing walk on the beach?"

My annoyance at Gaius's random appearance turned to gratitude when the nurse happily agreed while making googly eyes at him.

Gaius clapped his hands. "Wonderful! Now, let's make our way to the set before Duke plucks my feathers, shall we?"

"We wouldn't want that," Matteo said as he pulled back the white sheet to hop out of bed.

That was when I noticed that he was *only* wearing boxers under there. I gawked silently at the curve of his cock in his underwear and his toned, hairy legs before I wrenched my gaze away. I hurried out of the room before anyone saw my deeply flushed cheeks.

And as I did so, I realized something else.

During the whole time I spent with Matteo, I hadn't thought about Aquila once.

SEVEN

Matteo

DESPITE MY VISION being impeded by two black eyes, the beach was still gorgeous. The shimmering sunset turned the white sand golden, and the gentle ocean waves flowed back and forth on the shore in a comforting rhythm.

It was all perfect... except for the unholy amount of omegas crowding Thystle. The black eyes ended up being helpful since I could glare at them without anybody knowing.

When I regained consciousness after the brawl, I didn't expect to see an identical pair of curious alphas wearing weird hats. They had introduced themselves as Aurum and Saffron—Thystle's brothers. After the nurse chased them off, I figured I'd be alone until I got better... but then Thystle himself showed up at my door.

My heart skipped remembering the way he looked at me. Even before he spoke, I could tell he felt awful about the whole thing, even though none of it was his fault. The staff was responsible for the overcrowding, not him.

And then, when Thystle's entire face lit up during our conversation...

A pleasant shiver ran through me. His smile was so beautiful. It seared into my mind, a permanent memory of his joy.

As I watched him mingle with dozens of contestants, that genuine smile was absent. I could tell he was faking it to varying degrees of success. It mostly resembled an awkward grimace. Poor guy. I'd suggested to Alaric that Thystle might be more social than he assumed, but I was wrong. I'd bet $100 Thystle would rather have a root canal than talk to one more stranger.

But that didn't stop strangers from wanting to talk to *him*. Omega after omega swarmed Thystle, boasting and showing off as they clamored for his attention. I thought Alaric was desperate in the first season, but compared to these guys, he possessed the patience of a saint.

"This is ridiculous," the cat shifter in question grumbled beside me. We stood by the bar—which was securely staffed after the lobby incident—since neither of us wanted to breach the chaotic crowd. "How is anybody supposed to have quality one-on-one time with Thystle when the frat crew mobs him?"

I took a sip of my gin and tonic. It was a plain drink, just the way I liked it.

"Claw your way in?" I suggested.

"I seem to recall from a recent event that violence gets you kicked off the show," Alaric said wryly.

"Sure. But you'd make a killer impression," I joked.

Alaric heaved a dramatic sigh and asked the bartender for another shot of Baileys. After he threw it back, he huffed. "I told myself that after the first season, I'd take my time and play the long game. But at this rate, Thystle won't even remember who the hell I am."

"I mean this in the least offensive way possible, but you're hard to forget, Alaric."

He flashed a crooked grin. "And you're the opposite, Matteo. In the least offensive way possible, of course."

"None taken," I promised.

That was the goal, after all. To blend seamlessly into the background, never to be the center of attention again.

Though, I was starting to see a glitch in my strategy. In the short amount of time I'd known Thystle, I'd grown fond of him. And I was attracted to him—far, *far* more than I ever was to Crimson. A bud of hope whispered in my ear that maybe... he might be the one.

But if I inched my way closer to his heart, and if the feeling was mutual, wouldn't that thrust me directly into the limelight? The exact thing I was trying to avoid?

My warring feelings nagged at me. I couldn't shake the itchy, anxious feeling of standing out, yet I wanted to find my fated mate more than anything. In the end, my desire for love won out. That was why I accepted the invitation for season two.

I felt like I stood on the edge of a yawning chasm with everything I ever wanted beyond the terrifying pit. I couldn't live my whole life dodging the things that scared me. I had to take the leap of faith and fly.

Just as that thought entered my mind, I heard a loud voice addressing Thystle. I looked over to see a tall, jock-like omega looming over him, clearly trapping him in a conversation he didn't want to be in.

I was appalled at that man's behavior. In the first season of the Games, the omegas were polite and civil, waiting for Crimson to address them first. But many of the contestants here now were rowdy and downright rude.

I thrust my drink at Alaric, who took it with a confused frown.

"Where are you going?" he asked.

I almost said *to protect what's mine.* But I stopped myself at the last second before the words left my tongue.

Thystle wasn't mine. We'd only spoken once. Why was I so defensive over him? I dismissed the thought, blaming it on my compassionate nature. This was just like earlier, when I protected Muzo from that bully. I disliked it when people imposed their will on others. Nothing more.

"I'll be back in a minute," I said under my breath before storming off.

Thystle wasn't a huge alpha—he was an average height, toned, yet lithe and wiry. The jock omega was larger than him and used his size to his advantage, cutting off Thystle's escape route.

"You haven't spent *any* time with me yet," the omega complained. "Let's share a drink."

Thystle looked like a haggard substitute teacher dealing with too many obnoxious teenagers.

"I'm fine, thanks," he said curtly. He stepped around the omega, obviously trying to escape the crowd, but the man got in his way and raised his cup.

"C'mon, man, don't be like that. I came all this way to meet you," the omega said.

Poor Thystle. I could tell from his expression that he deeply regretted inviting so many people now.

"Sorry, I just need a second," Thystle mumbled, dodging the man in the other direction.

When the omega blocked his path a second time, I grew enraged.

Thanks to my ability to blend into the background, nobody noticed when I slipped next to the offending omega. By the time he *did* notice me, it was too late. I'd thrust myself between them like a brick wall.

"Matteo!" Thystle said.

The raw relief in his voice told me I'd done the right

thing. I was glad I trusted my instincts, even if they consistently got me into trouble with meatheads.

"Hey, dick," the omega barked. "I'm having a conversation here."

I held up a hand to show him I wasn't looking for a fight. "My apologies. I've got an urgent message for Thystle."

The man crossed his arms. He clenched his cup so hard the plastic started to crumple. "So tell him already."

"*Private* message," I amended. "Thystle, shall we?"

He nodded and played along. "Oh, yes. An urgent, private message. This must be important. Excuse me." We scurried away from the crowd and hid beneath a beach umbrella. When we were alone, Thystle let out an exhausted sigh.

"Holy Drake, I never want to do that again," he grumbled, then casually leaned against my shoulder. "How do extroverts exist?"

I blinked, pleasantly surprised he used me for support. Literally.

"Even an extrovert would get tired in *that* crowd," I remarked.

"Thanks for saving my life. I was actually about to walk out into the ocean if one more stranger talked to me."

"You're welcome. I was going to *escort* that man into the ocean if he didn't stop bothering you."

Thystle smirked. "Wow, you're darker than I thought. I like that in a man."

A cottony sensation fluttered in my chest. I didn't expect Thystle's flirty compliments. Did he do that with everybody, or only me?

I shrugged. "I couldn't stand around and do nothing while that man missed all your distress signals." Thystle tilted his head, glancing at my swollen eyes. "That's a running theme with you, huh? Can't ignore people in need?"

I grinned. "I suppose it is."

"Wow. Are you secretly some kind of hero? Or superstar?"

The ridge of my back went straight. He didn't know how close to the truth his words cut. I didn't let my surprise show on my face, instead giving him a soft laugh.

"Not at all. I'm just a regular person," I said.

My body felt shivery as Thystle continued to stare. He kept searching my face, almost as if looking for something specific. I tensed under his scrutiny.

He couldn't know, could he?

But then he sighed and lounged against me like a cat curling up on a sofa. "Well, anyway, I appreciate it. You're the only person here who seems to care about my feelings."

That fluttery sensation happened again. I *did* care about him. I was glad it came across.

"Can I ask you something?" I began.

"Sure."

"If you're so introverted, why'd you invite all these contestants?"

Thystle groaned and buried his face in my shoulder. The warmth of his breath against my skin sent a shiver down my spine.

"I can't tell you," he grumbled.

"Why not?"

"You're gonna think I'm really stupid."

"I would never think that."

Thystle glanced up at me for a long moment. His pale purple eyes were gorgeous up close, like the first lilac blossoms of spring.

"You know, when you say that, Matteo, I want to believe it."

I smiled slowly at him. "Good. I hope you do."

A tinge of pink bloomed on his pale cheeks. He cleared his throat and turned his face so I couldn't see it.

"Do you think any of them notice I'm missing?" he asked, nodding at the rambunctious crowd of omegas. They'd apparently grown bored and were now chanting something about "chugging". A couple security kobolds stood on standby, ready to defuse any drunken conduct. Since the bar staff were packing up, it was safe to assume the alcohol supply was officially cut off.

"No," I said. "Now answer *my* question."

"Can't a guy evade interrogation in peace?"

"Not after I saved your life," I teased.

He huffed. "Wow, blackmail much? You *are* dark. Is that why you dress like you're in the mafia?"

The comment blindsided me, making me choke into laughter. "What? I do not!"

"Yes, you do," Thystle argued flatly. "White shirt. Black pants. You're dressed like you've got something to hide."

I gawked at him. How could he be so right, yet so hilariously wrong? "I can assure you I'm not in the mafia," I said wryly. "And Taylor wore something similar back on season one. Well, before Crimson spilled soda all over his white shirt and stained it forever."

"My brother spilled a drink on Taylor?" Thystle blurted with a laugh. "Wow, he conveniently left that out in all his stories."

"You didn't watch the first show?" I asked.

"It's not my thing." He shuffled his feet. "But now I kind of wish I had. So I could see more of you."

Warmth suffused my chest.

"There wasn't much to see," I admitted. "I didn't perform particularly well in the challenges, and I didn't do anything memorable. Alaric was my fellow contestant, and he didn't even recall my name."

Thystle scowled. "Whatever. I'm gonna watch the episodes you're in. I'll fast-forward through all the other crap."

I was genuinely shocked. Why would he offer to do that? Was he just being nice? "You don't have to—"

Thystle sharply glanced at me. "I will. And that's the end of it."

The sudden twist of ferocity reminded me of who I was dealing with—an alpha dragon. A creature of supposed myth.

One who'd taken such a liking to me that he'd watch a full season of TV in which I was a mere background character just to see glimpses of me.

Something glinted in the corner of my eye. It was a reflection of light from the camera lens. I'd completely forgotten the Dragonfate Games were being filmed. Did the crew get our whole conversation?

Was I now a person of interest?

Paranoia surged through me. My muscles tensed. Because I was so comfortable around Thystle, I'd let my guard down. I hoped I hadn't said anything on film I'd regret later.

"Hey." Thystle's quiet voice pulled me out of my racing thoughts. "Don't worry about the cameras. Focus on me."

To drive his point home, he glared at the camera crew until they backed off. They'd have to be content with filming from afar.

Some of the tension left my shoulders. Thystle noticed my discomfort and acted instantly. It felt good that he'd looked out for me, the same way I did for him.

Did he share the way I felt about him, too? Judging by

the way he continued to lean on my shoulder, I wondered if that was the case...

The fluttering feeling in my chest could no longer be contained. It seeped throughout my limbs, making them tingly where Thystle touched me. I didn't want him to move. I wanted him to stay there, resting on me forever.

Without thinking, I raised my arm to put it around him. The urge felt natural. It felt *right*.

Just before my hand landed on him, someone cleared their throat, jolting both of us. We pulled apart.

At first I bristled, thinking it was the obnoxious jock omega from earlier. But it was a contestant I hadn't met yet. The man had slicked-back dark hair and sharp, cutting brown eyes. Unlike me, he had no issue looking flashy. His loosely buttoned shirt revealed the top half of his chest, and an expensive watch glinted on his wrist.

"Sorry to interrupt," he said with a bright white smile. "I'm Talon, one of the contestants."

The name shot into my brain like an arrow before I realized I was overreacting. The fact that it was half of TalonStorm was a coincidence. It was a common name among bird of prey shifters. He must've been a raptor of some sort.

Talon went on. "I couldn't help but notice our bachelor was missing, so I came to find him. Can't have a meet-and-greet without Thystle, can we?"

I searched Thystle's expression, wanting to know how he felt about the intrusion. But taking a break from the crowd seemed to afford him the mental stamina to greet someone new.

"Hey, Talon," he said. "Nice to meet you."

As they shook hands—which was a completely normal, polite thing to do—a hot rush of jealousy surged through me.

That's when I knew I was screwed. I was already off the deep end for Thystle.

"And you must be a fellow contestant," Talon said. His white smile continued to blind me. "Sorry we haven't met before. Big crowd, you know?"

"Yes," I said, trying not to sound too curt.

"And your name is?"

"Matteo."

Talon nodded, then appraised me. "What kind of shifter are you?"

Why did he want to know? Was he trying to get an edge on me in the following challenges? Or he was only curious, and I was overthinking it?

"Golden eagle," I replied.

Talon's brows rose. "What are the odds! I'm a Steller's sea eagle. We feathered folk better stick together in the challenges." He winked at Thystle. "Might give us an edge with the handsome bachelor, eh?"

At that moment, I was happy *not* to be in eagle form— all my feathers would've furiously puffed up, making me look like a raging harpy.

The hot envy coursing through my veins was unusual. I *never* got jealous. I was a calm, collected, down-to-earth person...

Until Thystle entered my life.

"Haha, yeah," Thystle said, though he didn't sound enthused. He faced me with a strained smile. "Guess I should go back and mingle with the crowd I invited, huh?"

Dammit, we hadn't even finished our conversation. I wished Talon hadn't shown up to interrupt us.

"Guess so," I agreed through my teeth.

Thystle lingered, watching my face. He seemed in no hurry to leave.

"Why don't you come with me?" he suggested. "Might be nice to have a bodyguard like before."

There was a playful edge in his voice, but it was also earnest. He *wanted* me to stand by his side. Hope flared within me. I didn't care that Talon's expression fell flat with disappointment. If Thystle wanted me there, I'd never refuse.

I flashed him a relieved smile. "I'd love to."

EIGHT

Thystle

AFTER THE CATEGORY five disaster that was the meet-and-greet, I was exhausted from that soul-sucking endeavor. I wanted to melt into my bed and fuse to it for the next year until I regained my energy. Whose thought-less idea was it to invite all those Drake-damned people?

Oh, right. It was mine.

Once the event ended and the producers ushered the omegas back to the hotel, I couldn't even move. As much as I wanted to, dragging myself back to my bedroom seemed beyond the scope of my abilities. I lazed on a beach recliner and stared up at the evening sky. I was too tired to even put on my headphones and listen to music. I needed silence.

How many new faces had I seen today? Definitely more than all the people I'd known in my entire life. I'd already forgotten most of their names, but a few stood out. The omegas from season one, I remembered hearing about from Crimson and Taylor. Alaric, that haughty cat; Poppy, the meek wolf; Muzo, the whimsical jackal...

Among the new faces, there was Talon, the snappily dressed sea eagle. Admittedly, his name intrigued me more than his personality. Was it just a coincidence that it was half of TalonStorm? He had brown eyes, too, like Aquila.

But Talon's eyes... they weren't right. The shape and color were correct, but something was missing, a *spark* that only Aquila ignited in me.

I sighed, rolling over on the recliner. My hand dangled in the sand. I drew little circles in it as my mind wandered... and landed on Matteo.

My hand froze. I'd drawn the shape of a golden eagle.

I sat up as my heart snagged, throwing in a few extra beats. Could I not even *think* about him without my chest getting all fluttery?

I turned towards the hotel. It was late enough that most contestants should've been asleep, especially considering the long day they'd had. But a good chunk of the rooms were still brightly lit. I guessed they were partying to make the most of their vacation. That's all this was to them. An all-expenses paid vacation. And honestly, I didn't even care. Let them party. I felt nothing towards most of those omegas except a mild annoyance that they were here, but that was my fault.

But there was *somebody* in the hotel who called to me. The urge simmered, then overflowed into a boil. It was impossible to ignore.

I stood up and took a slow step towards the building.

It wasn't the party crowd I wanted to see.

It was Matteo.

But how was I supposed to find him? I couldn't go in and ask the front desk, since I technically wasn't supposed to talk to the contestants after filming hours, and the thought of asking the partygoers made me shudder. Knocking on every door and waking everyone else up until I found him obviously wasn't an option, either.

I pulled out my robust flip phone. The twins made fun

of me for being stuck in the past—ten years ago to be precise—but I didn't give a crap about their opinions.

A weary, familiar voice answered. "Hello?"

"Hey, Taylor," I said. "I didn't wake you, did I?"

He yawned with his tiger's growl slipped into it. "No, I'm making sure Ruby doesn't yank Crimson's suits off their hangers. My mate would have a conniption fit."

I snorted, wishing I was there to see it.

"What's up?" Taylor asked. In the background, I heard Ruby's babbling and the rustling of coat hangers.

I shuffled on my feet. "Do you remember what Matteo's room number is?"

When Taylor spoke, I heard him grinning. "In the hotel? Sure, it's 328. Why?"

Heat rushed to my cheeks. Nothing got past him. But Taylor's knowledge that I liked Matteo was a small price to pay for his room number.

"Thanks, gotta go, bye," I mumbled hurriedly, then hung up.

Third floor. My gaze flew to the third floor on the outside of the building. All the rooms were brightly lit, their windows open and rowdy voices streaming out... except one. That must've been Matteo's room.

Magic flowed through me as I shifted. I slipped into my dragon form for a few moments to fly to his balcony, then promptly changed back to remain hidden. Nobody made a fuss. They must've been too busy partying to notice a giant purple dragon outside their windows.

Matteo's room was dark. His sliding door was slightly ajar to let in the night breeze. I felt bad for him. How could he sleep with this surrounding racket?

I quietly opened the door just enough to slip through. As I took my first step into Matteo's room, I paused.

Was this creepy? Yes.

Did I care? No.

Was that a bad sign? Maybe.

I didn't want to *do* anything weird to Matteo. I just wanted to look at him a little.

There he was, lying on his back in bed. His eyes were closed, and his chest rose and fell in a steady rhythm. I crept closer as my heart fired up. My dragon soul stirred, pleased with this situation. It liked that Matteo was asleep and vulnerable right in front of me...

Okay, maybe it was in my nature as a dragon to be inherently creepy. We were selfish, possessive creatures who guarded our things fiercely.

And I wanted Matteo to be *my thing*.

My footsteps fell silently on the carpet as I approached his bed. Matteo's poor eyes were still swollen from the fight. They were in the rough stage, where they got worse before they got better. But the rest of him was in fine shape. It pleased me to see him wearing something other than a stuffy white button-up shirt. The simple grey tank he wore to bed exposed his toned arms. He was no bodybuilder, but he wasn't a waif of an omega either. He was just right. Fit, healthy, and fertile...

The intrusive thought struck me like an arrow. I shook it off. Why was I thinking about *that?* I blew out a quiet breath, willing the sudden rush of heat to leave my cheeks.

I came to look. That was all. So, I looked. I looked at his gorgeous face, marred by the unfortunate black eyes. I looked at his strong nose, his high cheekbones, his jawline peppered with stubble, the bob of his Adam's apple as he breathed in and out...

I was riveted. I couldn't stop staring at him. Like, *literally* could not stop. My eyes objected to every attempt to gaze somewhere else. My own body rebelled against me.

The only other time I'd felt this way was about my Aquila poster, and even that paled in comparison to this.

As I stared like a madman at Matteo's closed, puffy eyes, it struck me that I'd never seen them *not* swollen. What did they look like? Excitement thrummed as I recalled my promise to watch the first season of the Dragonfate Games. Then I'd know exactly. But watching the show meant leaving Matteo's room, and I didn't want to go. I wanted to stay here with him until daybreak.

A familiar obsession swirled inside me. This was just like with Aquila, except Matteo was a real flesh-and-blood person. He was an omega contestant on *my* show. He was in my reach. He could be mine.

My hand rose on its own and reached forward. As my palm landed gently on Matteo's cheek, electric jolts flew up to my shoulder. My skin tingled. My heart leapt into my throat. Growing bolder, I moved my thumb along his soft cheek. It felt so nice to touch him. I almost wished he was awake to feel it, too.

"Hi, Thystle," Matteo murmured.

The warmth in my blood turned to ice. My hand froze in place. Right against Matteo's cheek.

He didn't say that, right? I was hallucinating. He was still asleep, because his eyes were still— Oh. They weren't closed anymore. He was looking straight at me.

Embarrassment shimmied up my spine, flooding me with shame. This would be a great time for the hotel floor-boards to break.

When I tried to retract my hand, I couldn't. Matteo's fingers curled around my wrist, keeping my hand there. I felt dizzy.

"Um," I said. "Hi."

He smiled, even though he had no business smiling

since a dragon just broke into his room and creepily touched his sleeping face.

"I thought you were asleep," I admitted.

He angled his head towards the sliding door. "I was trying to be. But it's pretty loud."

I felt the blood drain from my face. "So... you were awake this whole time?"

"Yes."

"Great. Amazing," I muttered, slapping my other hand over my face.

Matteo chuckled. "You seem upset."

"I'm not upset. I'm just an idiot."

"I fail to see how."

"Gee, how about we start with breaking and entering into the room of a guy who's fully conscious?"

"If I'd been unconscious, it would've also been bad," Matteo teased.

He should've been mad. Why wasn't he mad? Why was he taking this so damn well? Flustered, I blew out a breath. "Do you *like* that I'm here?"

A slow grin spread over Matteo's mouth. "I'm not opposed to it. It felt nice when you touched my face."

My temperature skyrocketed. I hadn't just broken into his room, I'd *stroked* him—while he was awake the entire time. The creep-meter was pegging hard.

Or at least, it should've been—except Matteo was totally into it. Hell, he'd grabbed my arm to prevent me from leaving.

"You know, I'm technically not allowed to be here," I reminded him.

"Sure. But you're here now. What am I supposed to do, chase you away?" he joked.

"That *is* fully within your right," I mumbled.

He tilted his head, gazing up at me. "And so is allowing

you to stay."

Heat flooded my cheeks. The way he looked at me, combined with his firm hand on my wrist, elicited a strange, fluttery feeling in my chest. The closest sensation was how I felt when I listened to Aquila's songs. But this was different. It was immediate and visceral, like sticking my hand into an open flame versus sitting by a cozy campfire.

And I wanted to keep jumping into the flames over and over again.

"If that's what *you* want," I said slowly, "then I'll stay."

My heart pounded in my throat. It was Matteo's suggestion, but fuck, I wanted it so badly. I didn't care if it was selfish. The only way I'd leave his room was if he told me to get out.

Matteo smiled. "Good."

When he shuffled over in the bed and patted the space next to him, my jaw dropped.

"I—I was going to sleep on the floor," I said.

Matteo scoffed. "Really, Thystle? We're not teenagers at our first sleepover. Come here."

I stared at the empty half of the bed. "This is *so* against the rules."

"You already broke them," Matteo reminded me dryly. "So you may as well enjoy yourself."

My heart did back flips as I edged towards the mattress. The fact that this was forbidden made it feel so good.

And *fuck*, the whole bed smelled amazing. Matteo's scent was all over it.

I couldn't resist for a second longer. I was about to climb into bed when Matteo asked, "You're going to sleep dressed like that?"

Blushing, I shot back, "What, do you want me to

strip?"

He shrugged. "It's odd to go to bed fully clothed, don't you think? Sleep like you usually do."

The temperature steadily rose in my cheeks. "I sleep in my underwear."

Matteo grinned. "So do I."

I gave up. With a huff, I kicked off my pants and shirt, then climbed into bed beside him, not giving a shit what rules I broke.

"Was that so hard?" Matteo asked.

"No. But if Duke finds out, he'll skin my hide."

He chuckled, resting his head against the pillow. "He'll have to go through me first. And trust me, you don't want to fight a pissed off eagle. Our talons aren't for show."

He'd do that for me? I thought.

"Speaking of talons, the first challenge is tomorrow, huh?" I mused. "That Talon guy is gonna be there."

As soon as I mentioned the name, Matteo's eyes flashed. Despite the swelling, I could tell they'd grown sharp and hard.

Was he... jealous?

"That's right," Matteo said in a clipped tone. "If he thinks we're somehow allied because we're both eagles, he's in for a surprise."

Yeah. Totally jealous. That was a side of Matteo I hadn't seen yet and didn't expect. He was such a cool guy that it amused me to see this facet of him.

I grinned. "Don't worry, you've got the edge on everyone. You have experience from being on the show before."

Matteo smirked. "True."

He had an extra edge, too—the fact that I liked him. But I felt too shy to share that. I was already in Matteo's bed. It might make things weird if I confessed to crushing on him.

That jealous aura continued to mill above his head. As adorable as it was, I didn't want him to worry, so I scooted closer reassuringly. His shoulders relaxed. That seemed to calm him down.

"Hey," I said. "Is this weird? Be honest."

The corner of Matteo's mouth curled up. "You'll have to be specific, because plenty about this situation is weird."

"You know what I mean. That I'm in your bed."

He sighed in amusement, like I was being silly. "Look at it this way. I'm one of dozens of omega contestants on a private island being filmed for a reality TV dating show in which *you*, an alpha dragon, are the prize. The fact that you're lying in bed with me is the least weird part about all this."

I blushed furiously. "Well, when you put it that way..."

To my surprise, Matteo put his arm around me. I sucked in a soft breath. The sudden touch made my skin hot and tingly all over.

"Thystle, if you're weird, I don't ever want you to be normal," Matteo murmured.

If the warm touch wasn't bad enough, his beautiful, comforting words were the final nail in the coffin. I was head over heels for Matteo and the Dragonfate Games had barely begun.

I exhaled sharply, because if I didn't, I would've broken into a big, stupid smile, and I didn't want to embarrass myself like that over a few nice words.

"Are you always this mushy?" I asked, hiding my face from him.

"Why? You don't like it?" he teased.

"Didn't say that," I mumbled under my breath. "If you're trying to get a head start in the Games, you're doing a decent job."

"Thystle, I don't care about the Games," he said

mildly. "If I have to participate in the challenges, then so be it. But I'm only here to find my fated mate. That's all."

My heartbeat rampaged. He was so earnest, it was painful. He wasn't like the people I'd met tonight chasing the fame of being on a popular TV show, or the glory of courting an alpha dragon. Matteo was here for love. For the mate destined for him.

What if that was me?

A firm knock came from the hallway, followed by the irritated voice of hotel staff ordering the partying neighbors to quiet down. They argued for a moment, then reluctantly obeyed. The floor went silent after that.

"Guess that's our cue to finally go to sleep," Matteo remarked.

"Thank Holy Drake," I mumbled. "I'm never gonna stop regretting inviting all these damned people."

Matteo arched a sly brow at me. "Don't think you've escaped that conversation, by the way. When we're awake, I expect a real answer this time."

I snorted. For some reason, I liked that he dogged me about it. "Fine. I owe you."

He smiled, then closed his eyes. "Goodnight, Thystle."

"Night."

I thought he'd turn around to sleep, but he lay on his back, giving me a full view of his sleeping face. Was he teasing me, or was I reading too much into it? Dammit, having a crush was impossible.

Since Matteo didn't turn around, I didn't either. I retained my position curled up beside him with my head on the spare pillow.

I didn't fall asleep right away. My dragon soul wouldn't let me. Instead I spent half an hour burning every inch of Matteo's face into my memory before I was finally content, then I drifted off.

NINE

Matteo

WHEN I WOKE the next morning, Thystle was still there.

An intense feeling of warmth and joy seeped through me as I gazed upon his resting face. In sleep, he looked so peaceful and calm. He didn't wear the prickly mask he showed to the world. When he was asleep, he could just *be*.

A smile spread across my face as I remembered what happened last night. I didn't regret playing possum and pretending to be asleep. Thystle's 'crime' was downright adorable. Honestly, it flattered me that he'd broken the rules because he wanted to see me.

And when I recalled the sensation of his gentle hand on my face... I shuddered. How sweet, how light of a touch he had. Who knew alpha dragons could be so tender?

I glanced at the digital clock on the bed stand. On a normal day, I would've been out of bed by now. In fact, I should've gotten up half an hour ago. Today was the first challenge of the games. I couldn't be late. But Thystle's siren song captured me. I didn't want to leave him. This early morning coziness was a feeling I could definitely get used to.

I gazed at him fondly. His thin layer of black eyeliner smeared against the pillow, and his wispy lavender and purple hair spilled over his face like a curtain of wisteria flowers.

An urge overcame me. I reached over and brushed the hair off his cheek, letting my thumb drag against it gently. His skin was soft in that particular way that only occurred during sleep.

My heart thrummed. Right now, I felt more like a hummingbird than an eagle, fluttery and delicate.

Thystle made a soft sound, but didn't awaken. I was surprised my touch didn't rouse him. He was more honest than me, who faked it just to see what would happen.

But my fake sleep last night wasn't the only thing I kept from Thystle.

I bit my lip. I didn't want to lie to him, but I also didn't want the truth to come out. Was that too much to ask? I caressed Thystle's cheek in a slow rhythm. As I stared into his peaceful face, a great sense of determination came over me. Thystle trusted me. I had to have the same faith in him. I made a vow to tell him the truth, no matter how much it terrified me.

But not right now. Thystle was exhausted from yesterday's events, so I let him sleep. Besides, he seemed to be having a good dream, if the slight smile in the corner of his mouth was any indication.

Before I chickened out, I leaned over and pressed a tiny kiss to his forehead then slipped out of bed to face the day.

Leaving Thystle to participate in the games was decidedly less pleasant than waking up beside him.

I expected a headache when I arrived at the location, and my suspicion was correct. Although the number of contestants had been whittled down thanks to the alcohol-related incidents, there were still far too many of them present. The beach felt crowded and sweaty from all the bodies.

As we waited for the last few contestants to arrive, I looked around. Gaius stood before us with a chipper smile, ready to announce the challenge. It wasn't hard to guess what it was. Large rings stood on the sand and were hung in the air via tall poles.

"Oh good," Alaric said as he strode up beside me. "Thystle is making us literally jump through hoops for him."

Despite his consistent stream of snarky comments, I was glad to have a familiar face nearby.

"I don't think Thystle chooses the challenges," I remarked.

"How do you know?" Alaric demanded.

"He didn't mention anything about an obstacle course."

Alaric raised a brow. "You spoke to him about it? When?"

Crap. I had to curb Alaric's suspicion—not for my sake, but for Thystle's. I didn't want him to get in trouble for meeting me after hours. *Could* he even get in trouble? He had the final say in everything, after all. Either way, I didn't push my luck.

"I brought it up during the meet-and-greet," I said casually. It wasn't true, of course, but I sincerely doubted this was Thystle's idea. This type of challenge wasn't his style.

Alaric took my comment at face value. As his aura of suspicion vanished, I thanked my ability to blend into the background. Not only were people quick to forget about me, they also assumed I was honest. Because honesty was boring.

"Wow, an obstacle course!" Muzo exclaimed.

"Oh dear, an obstacle course…" Poppy murmured at the same time.

The canine shifters appeared as a pair. I grinned at their polar opposite reactions. It was sweet how two very different people could be close friends.

"Looks like it," I said. "There're rings on the ground and in the air for every type of shifter."

Muzo bounded on the balls of his feet. "This is so cool. I love jumping through hoops!"

"I'll try my best, but I hope I don't knock them over by accident," Poppy said, fiddling with his hands.

Alaric sighed and rubbed his temple. "Dogs…"

Shortly after Muzo and Poppy's appearance, Gaius cleared his throat, flashed a brilliant grin, and began his announcement.

"Greetings, everyone, and welcome to the first challenge of the Dragonfate Games!"

Half the contestants roared in excitement, cheering and whooping. It sounded more like a football stadium than a private beach.

Alaric made a disgusted sound. "Those meatheads are giving me a migraine before we even start…"

I didn't reply, but I privately agreed with him. I couldn't be too harsh on them, though. None of them were Thystle's type. They never had a chance with him. Not that I was complaining.

Speaking of Thystle, where was he? I didn't see him anywhere. In the first season of the Games, Crimson accompanied Gaius at the start of every challenge. But Gaius was alone this time. Maybe they changed up the formula, and Thystle watched from afar.

I usually wasn't so competitive, but the need to win burned inside me. I wanted Thystle to see me do well.

"Your challenge today is a timed obstacle course

through these hoops," Gaius said, gesturing to the rings. "Not only will you race to the finish line, but you'll need to rack up points by going through the rings. The contestant with the fastest time and most points will be the winner!"

Something about Gaius's phrasing felt off. He'd said *the* winner. In the first season, we entered a pool of winners from which Crimson had the final say—and his choice was always Taylor, obviously. Even if Taylor hadn't come in the first place during the challenge, he still won in the end. But Gaius made it sound like there could only be one true winner this time—the person who came in first place.

Now, my competitive urge blazed into a wildfire. If that was true, I had to win. There was no other option.

Thystle *would* choose me.

"How many other flying shifters are here, I wonder?" Talon asked.

His sudden comment made my spine stiffen. I hadn't noticed his arrival. How long had he been standing there?

"I don't know," I replied honestly. "We're the only ones I'm aware of."

Talon glanced up at the sky rings. "Who's faster, I wonder?"

"I wouldn't know."

Talon sent a sidelong glance my way. "Guess we'll find out."

Was he taunting me? Or was this friendly competition I was taking the wrong way? I stared back at him, trying to gauge the look in his eyes, but Talon was difficult to read. Either that, or I didn't care enough to figure it out. I wasn't here to make friends. I was here to find my fated mate.

And I suspected I'd already found him.

"Contestants!" Gaius called. "You may now shift into your animal forms!"

My body changed in a flash. Rich brown feathers

erupted across my skin, my feet curled into powerful talons, and my mouth became a sharp, hooked beak. I unfurled my powerful wings, ready to launch myself into the sky on Gaius's mark.

My vision improved a hundredfold. On either side of me, I saw rows of shifters. I recognized the white house cat, arctic wolf, and black-backed jackal beside me. The other side were all strangers. My real competition.

On my right stood another eagle. Talon. His eagle form was starkly different from mine, with a distinct prominent beak and white markings. A flashier form to suit a flashier man.

I couldn't help a surge of bitterness flowing through me. I'd given up looking flashy in human form a long time ago. Talon reminded me of my past in a way that left a bad taste in my mouth.

"Ready..." Gaius called.

"Good luck, Matteo," Talon said under his breath.

The feathers on my neck ruffled. Did he really mean that, or was he playing mind games with me?

"GO!" Gaius shouted.

I rocketed upwards, beating my wings hard. Fiery determination surged through my muscles. I wouldn't lose.

The first ring hung ahead. All I had to do was fly through the rings as fast as possible. No problem. Despite living in a human city, I was an experienced flyer. Unlike wolves or tigers, it was easy for me to sneak away to spread my wings—figuratively and literally. Humans didn't bat an eye at a brown bird, especially not one thirty feet in the air.

As I neared the first ring, I tucked my wings close to my body to make myself more aerodynamic. I shot through the ring like a bullet. Free from it, I unfurled my wings again to fly towards the next one.

I heard loud flapping behind me. With his bulk, Talon struggled to keep up.

I scanned the beach. The four-legged shifters on the beach stormed the obstacle course, but their paws and hooves slowed on sand. None of them were as far along as me.

That meant *I* was in the lead.

A strange high washed over me. It felt familiar, like the presence of an old friend. It bubbled and welled up in my chest until it overflowed in a loud, sharp victory cry.

That's when I realized what the high was. It was the same feeling as being on stage, singing my throat raw, spilling my heart out in front of a screaming, adoring crowd.

The recognition shocked me. I faltered, stalling in mid-air.

It had been so long... Why did I feel this way now? And why did it feel so good?

A wing crashed into mine. The momentum sent me into a tailspin. I gasped and caught my bearings, flapping desperately to stay afloat.

Talon flew ahead. Did he hit me on purpose? He didn't stop to check if I was okay.

But now *he* was in the lead. Fury set my blood on fire. I darted behind him, flying as fast as my wings could carry me. He wasn't going to win. I wouldn't let him.

Urgency drove me forward. I was in a frenzy, determined to beat Talon and win this challenge. Was Thystle watching? Did he see how badly I wanted this?

I wanted to look for him, but there was no time. I couldn't spare a second to scan the beach when Talon was still in front of me. He ducked through the next ring, folding his wings the same way I did, then used gravity to his advantage to dive into the ring below it.

I cursed. His bulky size hindered him during lift off, but it was an asset now. I couldn't catch up to him.

The finish line was ahead. My heart sank. Talon was a whole wingspan away. If I didn't close the gap between us now, it would be too late.

Gaius got closer each second. He clutched a stopwatch in his hand, watching both land and sky eagerly for the winner to cross the finish line.

I pushed my body to its limit. Fire burned agonizingly in my muscles. I clenched my eyes shut through the pain. A few more wing strokes—

"TIME!" Gaius called.

I sucked in air and my eyes snapped open. Had I done it? I floated down to the sand where the rest of the exhausted land shifters panted for breath. I didn't see Talon. Hope fluttered in my chest. Was he still behind me?

"Who won, Gaius?" I asked.

Gaius wore an odd expression that set me on edge. His mask of confidence would fool most people, but I wasn't most people. I recognized a fellow liar hiding the truth.

"Why don't we wait for everyone to catch their breath first?" Gaius said, flashing a grin that failed to comfort me.

I realized Thystle still wasn't here. Did that have anything to do with Gaius's weird behavior?

"Gaius," I said firmly, glaring at him with my eagle eyes, "announce the winner."

His brows rose. He seemed taken aback by my sudden personality change, but I didn't care. I had to know.

Gaius summoned the closest member of the camera crew. "Can we double-check the film?"

The kobold nodded and showed Gaius a small screen. His face paled. He glanced distractedly at the stopwatch in his fist.

My feathers puffed up in anger. If he didn't tell me I'd won soon, I'd shred that stopwatch to pieces.

Gaius looked around, as if searching for someone, then cleared his throat and injected some enthusiasm into his voice. "All right! The winner of the first challenge is..."

My heart thudded, ruffling the downy feathers on my chest.

"Talon!"

I stopped breathing.

A victorious cry pierced the sky above me. Dread consumed me as I glanced up to see Talon circling above the beaten contestants in a victory lap.

Loud groans sounded among the crowd. Some complained loudly about how unfair the challenge was for land shifters, which made me angrier that I'd lost.

I should've won. Not Talon.

Poppy slumped next to me, putting his head on his paws in defeat. "That was so hard... But you did really well, Matteo."

His gentle voice yanked me out of my furious headspace.

"Thank you, Poppy," I said quietly.

Muzo sighed and collapsed on top of Poppy's back in a dogpile. His tongue lolled out of his mouth. "Geez, that was rough. There's so much sand between my paw pads. You were lucky you got to fly over it."

I didn't feel lucky at all.

Surprisingly, Alaric mirrored my feelings. He hissed as he padded closer, lifting his dainty white paws to avoid touching the hot sand. "He's *not* lucky. None of us are. We lost."

Muzo tilted his head. "Yeah, but we tried our best."

"Who cares?" Alaric spat. "Only the winner is important. Do you even know why you're on this island?"

"Uhh—"

"To find a fated mate. Nothing else matters."

"I was gonna say that," Muzo mumbled, his ears flattening against his head.

From the corner of my eye, I saw Talon gloating and thanking Gaius for announcing him the winner. I caught Gaius's awkward expression as he congratulated Talon.

What was going on? Why did Gaius choose the winner instead of Thystle? And where the hell *was* he? A thought struck me like lightning. The image of a peaceful Thystle floated into my mind.

There was no way he'd overslept and missed the challenge... right?

TEN

Thystle

EVERYTHING WAS SOFT. Warm. Comfortable. I never wanted to move.

A slow exhale left my lips as I nestled against the downy pillow. Cozy was an understatement. I was halfway to becoming one with the mattress itself.

As I inched closer to consciousness, I became sharply aware of Matteo's scent. It surrounded me like a soothing blanket. I breathed it in, then sucked in deep lungfuls, suddenly hungry for it.

Heat stirred between my legs. The fuzzy, horny feeling manifested in a growing erection.

I wriggled closer to Matteo's pillow, where his scent was the strongest, then buried my face in it. An electric jolt zapped down my spine.

Fuck, it smelled amazing.

I groaned, rubbing my face against his pillow, breathing in as much of his addictive scent as possible. It enticed me, allured me. My lips parted as I panted in choppy breaths. My cock hardened until it brushed against the mattress, sending a burst of arousal through my blood in a heady feedback loop.

I lost myself in my obsession with it. Dazed, I bucked my hips against the bed and sniffed Matteo's scent. It was sweet as honey, earthy as the ground after rain, and utterly drool-worthy.

In the back of my mind, I wondered what time it was. I had the vague memory that I had somewhere to be, but Matteo's aroma rooted me to the spot. No way could I escape it—nor did I want to. I was blissfully unaware of the rest of the world as I rubbed my face against his pillow, flooding my brain with his scent...

The key card clicked at the door.

Right. Matteo wasn't in bed, so he must've left. Had he returned? My heart skittered in excitement.

I opened my eyes just in time to see Matteo stride into the room. His usually tamed hair was mussed up, as if strenuous exercise had thrown it out of place, and his face was drawn in a tense way. Despite all that, his eyes flashed warmly when he saw me. The swelling remained, but had gone down considerably, giving me a clearer view of them. They were gorgeous.

But before I had the chance to study them, Matteo let out a breath and gave me a tired smile. "Good morning, Thystle. Or should I say good afternoon?"

I blinked. "Huh?"

"It's three PM."

I frowned, pulling myself up on my elbows. "It can't be."

Convinced he was wrong, I glanced at the digital clock. It *was* three PM.

Holy fucking Drake. Had I really spent all morning —*and* half the afternoon—smelling Matteo's pillow? Matteo slid onto the edge of the bed and grinned. In the few moments he was in the room, his mood had noticeably improved.

"You look happy. Did something happen?" he asked.

"N-no," I mumbled. There was no way I'd admit to my crimes. First breaking and entering, now this. "What about you? You looked unhappy until a couple seconds ago."

Matteo let out a rueful laugh. "You're sharp, aren't you? You're right. I do feel better seeing a cute dragon in my bed."

A blush seared my already warm cheeks. Being called *cute* also reminded me of the boner between my thighs. I doubted it would go away now that Matteo was here in the flesh. I had to stay hidden beneath the blanket so he didn't notice.

Something nagged at the back of my mind. Why did it feel like I was forgetting something? Oh well. Whatever it was couldn't be more important than sharing this private moment with Matteo. I liked this whole being-away-from-the-cameras thing.

Matteo tilted his head, looking at me fondly. It made my heart soar.

"You slept through it," he remarked.

"Through what?" I asked, too busy ogling him to think about it.

"The first challenge."

Wait.

What?

I gawked, scrambling upright in bed. "What? No, there's no way."

The corner of his mouth curled. "Where do you think I've been this whole time?" he asked wryly.

I had no response to that. In my half-sleepy, half-horny daze, I hadn't even thought about it.

"Shit, I'm sorry," I mumbled. "What happened?"

Matteo's gaze drifted down for a moment before flitting back up. I remembered my clothing situation was compromised. I was dressed only in my underwear, and since I'd leapt upright, my erection was exposed. I yanked the blanket over myself with a furious blush.

Matteo eyed my now-exposed boner and chuckled. "Don't worry. Morning wood happens."

Sexy, though it was, I pointedly ignored that statement.

"What happened at the challenge?" I asked through my teeth.

Matteo's jaw tightened. His gaze slid away from me, staring at the wall. "Talon won."

A flurry of rage swirled in my belly. "What? Who decided that?"

"Gaius did, since you weren't there," Matteo said. "I think he felt he had no choice."

I groaned. I was annoyed at the situation but mostly pissed at myself. How could I let this happen? My time as the bachelor of the Dragonfate Games was disastrous so far. Could I do *anything* right?

"Shit, I am so sorry," I mumbled. "I wanted to be there, I swear. I just..."

He cocked his head. "Overslept?" he offered.

I ran my hand through my messy bedhead. "Yeah. What was even the challenge? How'd Talon win?"

I didn't miss the flash of annoyance across Matteo's face. "It was an obstacle course. We had to rack up points while racing to the finish line."

My nose wrinkled. "That's stupid. Who the hell decided that?"

He smiled. "That's what I thought."

"Huh?"

"Alaric made a fuss about the challenge, saying it was odd you'd chosen it. But I knew you wouldn't pick something like that."

I sighed. "Yeah, I wouldn't. How the fuck is an obstacle course even supposed to help me find my fated mate?"

Matteo chuckled. "If you wanted to find the fittest, fastest mate, I suppose it's not the worst idea."

I rolled my eyes. "No, thanks. Jocks aren't my type."

"Who is your type?" Matteo challenged, meeting my gaze. Fire simmered in his molten brown eyes.

My breath caught in my throat. There was a clear answer to his question—he was sitting right in front of me. But I couldn't string the right words together.

Matteo took my silence as an invitation to continue. "What's the prize for winning the first challenge, anyway?" he asked, an edge to his tone.

I narrowed my eyes at him, then smirked. "You're pissed Talon won, aren't you, Matteo?"

His mouth became a thin line. "No."

I barked out a laugh. "Oh, come on. You're such a bad liar. Just admit it."

His brow twitched. "Am I?"

Suddenly, Matteo leaned in. He was close enough that his breath ghosted across my face, and the salty scent of his sweat filled my nose. My instincts flared to life.

Shit. I still hadn't fully come down from my earlier high. A fresh whiff of Matteo's scent was enough to drive me crazy.

But I was no pushover, either. I was an alpha dragon, and Matteo's playful challenge pricked at my desire to fight back.

I grinned, inching closer to meet him halfway. "Yeah, you are. You're pissed Talon won."

"Fine," he admitted without backing off. "I am. I should've won. Not him."

"Why do you want to win so badly?"

His gaze turned stormy. "You know why."

Oh, yeah. I *liked* this side of him. I liked him feisty and jealous and willing to act wild with me.

"I don't," I lied.

Matteo's smirk was a cutting crescent moon. He didn't tear his intense gaze off mine. "You broke into my room, overslept in *my* bed, and now you have the audacity to play dumb?"

A shiver shimmied up my spine. This was new—and fuck, it was *hot.* I'd underestimated Matteo. I knew there was a different side to him when we first met, but I didn't expect this.

"You gonna let me get away with it?" I asked in a husky voice.

Matteo stared at me for a long moment, during which my heart raced a mile a minute. I was convinced he heard it thudding against my ribs.

"No, I don't think I should," he said quietly.

I assumed the sudden softness of his tone indicated he was backing off—but the next second, Matteo snatched my wrists and pinned me to the bed.

My dragon soul roared to life. Heat burned in my whole body, from the ends of my hair down to the tips of my toes.

Yes, *yes.* This was so right.

Matteo's grip was firm but gentle. He knew I could've thrown him off in a second, but I sure as hell didn't want to. His face hovered above mine.

"I'm cashing in that explanation you owe me. Don't think I forgot," he said.

I let out a breathy laugh. "You've got me pinned to the bed and *that's* what you want? I can't believe you're still thinking about that."

"Eagles don't forget."

"I thought that was elephants."

Matteo scoffed and rocked his hips so he tipped forward. His lips were so close, I could touch them if I leaned up just a little...

"Cough it up, Thystle," he ordered. "You've spent the entirety of the Games so far avoiding most of the contestants, yet you were the one who invited them all. There's a reason. Tell me why."

Crap.

One way to kill the mood was to confess my embarrassing reasoning for summoning a hoard of contestants. But if I had to tell anybody, I didn't mind telling Matteo. Out of everyone I knew, I trusted him the most with this delicate confession.

"You have to promise not to make fun of me," I said.

"When have I ever?" he asked seriously.

"You might now. It's that stupid."

"Try me."

Something about Matteo's weight straddling my waist comforted me. He was like a living weighted blanket.

"Do you know the band TalonStorm?" I asked.

Matteo froze. It looked like he stopped breathing. For a second, I grew excited, thinking he might be a fellow super fan, but my hopes were dashed when he tilted his head back and forth in a so-so gesture.

"I've heard of them before," he said slowly.

Oh well. There was plenty of time to teach him later.

"Anyway, they're only my favorite band of all time," I said, unable to stop the eagerness that crept into my voice. "I have all their albums on CD and vinyl—even the special editions—and, like, every piece of merch they ever put out."

Matteo's brows rose a fraction. "You do?"

I broke into a grin. "I'll show you. It's all safely stashed away in my hoard."

"That's... impressive." Matteo smiled slightly. "I'd love to see it."

A burst of joy exploded in my chest. Matteo wanted to see my TalonStorm collection. He was *actually* interested in my hoard.

"I could grab you and kiss you right now," I blurted out.

Matteo blinked, then broke into laughter. "Do you say that to every man who sees your hoard?"

My cheeks burned from my sudden outburst, but his comment brought me down to earth. "No. Dragons' hoards are special. Private. We don't just show them to anybody. Only people we really trust."

His expression turned gentle. "I see. I'm flattered. But that still doesn't explain your reasoning," he teased.

I blew out a dramatic sigh. Screw my shame, I'd get it over with since he wouldn't stop asking.

"Fine. I'm obsessed with the lead singer of Talon-Storm, and even though nobody's seen him in a decade, I wanted him to be on the show because I was convinced he's my fated mate. Happy now? I told you it was stupid and embarrassing."

Matteo stared into the middle distance, like his soul had left his body. For a second, he didn't seem fully present in the room.

My heart sank. Oh no. Was this like the Talon thing? Had I upset him by bringing up another man again? "Please don't take it the wrong way," I said hurriedly. "I told you it was embarrassing. It's just a dumb crush I've had since I was sixteen."

Matteo shook it off, breaking into a shaky smile. "No, Thystle, it's okay."

That's what he said, but he still looked frazzled. My dragon instincts rumbled at me to claim Matteo. I threw my arms around his neck, capturing him. I didn't want him to run away because I'd said something wrong.

"Stay," I said.

Matteo exhaled in amusement. His loose body language indicated he wasn't going anywhere. "This is my room, remember? Why would I leave?"

"I thought you were upset," I mumbled.

He shook his head. "Not at all, but thank you for thinking of me."

Relieved, I relaxed against the bed. Being underneath him was a nice feeling.

But what did being on *top* of him feel like?

With my embarrassing confession and the awkward tension out of the way, I remembered the arousal between my thighs. Matteo's looming position wasn't helping in that regard.

My arms still looped around his shoulders. I shivered at the heat of his skin and the prickling hairs on the back of his neck. He held still, like he was holding back.

Well, screw that.

"Matteo," I murmured. "I should've been there at the first challenge. Let me make it up to you."

His still-swollen eyes widened. "Oh? What exactly do you have in mind?"

"I'm sure you can guess."

His lip curled into a smirk. "This game again?"

"You'll like the game this time."

And in one fluid motion, I flipped him over. Now I was on top—and I had him *exactly* where I wanted him.

ELEVEN

Matteo

I WAS CONVINCED he was my fated mate.

Thystle's words echoed in my head. His confession stunned me. I felt like I'd taken a brick to the face. Maybe two.

Thystle was obsessed with Aquila? As in, my alter-ego, Aquila?

He'd orchestrated the Games, and invited this horde of people...just to meet *me?*

I would've laughed at the irony if Thystle hadn't been drop-dead serious. I saw the light sparkle in his eyes as he gushed earnestly over TalonStorm. He was honest-to-gods in love with Aquila.

That was what it was. Love. He'd called it obsession, but he downplayed it because he didn't want me to be jealous. He was sweet that way.

Little does he know...

It wasn't obsession. Knowing how Thystle gazed fondly into my eyes, the kind way he spoke to me, the way he'd do anything for me—it could only be love.

And if that was true, it meant Thystle had been in love with me for the past ten years.

I could almost commend fate on this ironic twist. Well played, you minx.

But I didn't have time to dwell on that revelation. I was so turned on by Thystle's sudden advance that I couldn't think straight anymore.

The air left my lungs as Thystle took control. His average size belied his lightning speed and secret strength. He was an alpha dragon. I'd do well to remember that.

He'd reversed our positions in one fell swoop, like a predator hunting its prey. As an apex predator myself, I wasn't used to being on this end of the chase, but I liked it. Thystle's intense gaze sent shivers down my spine. He stared at me like I was the only thing in the world.

"You look good down there," he said. His silky hair fell around his face in a purple curtain, making him look sensual and intimidating in the sexiest way possible.

"And you look good on top of me," I shot back.

I glanced at his lower half. His erection was hard to miss. I'd noticed it the second the covers dropped from his body. But now it was harder than ever, tenting his underwear. It made my mouth water.

And my mouth wasn't the only reactive part of my body. Beneath all my clothes, my hole twitched. Thystle's playful dominance stirred my omega instincts. I wasn't one to bow to an alpha's will, but Thystle was... special. His act of flipping me over and straddling my waist was enough to arouse me. I wondered if he smelled my scent the same way I drank in his. His spicy, musky aroma was softened by sleep, yet it assaulted my nostrils and fiercely turned me on.

"You smell so good," I murmured.

Thystle grinned like he was about to indulge me in a secret. "Do you know what I was doing in your bed before you showed up?"

An anticipatory shudder jolted across my skin.

"Tell me," I said.

Thystle leaned closer so our cheeks nearly touched, then whispered, "I was sniffing your pillow and grinding against your bed."

I groaned. That mental image went straight to my cock.

"So, that's why you were hard when I walked in," I remarked.

"There was no hiding it..."

"Don't hide," I said. "I like seeing you."

His grin widened. "I'd hope so, since you're a contestant in the Games."

I scowled. "Forget the damned Games. I want *you*, Thystle, competition or not."

He paused for a second, a hopeful expression fleetingly crossing his face. "Is that why you're so mad Talon won the first challenge?"

"Keep bringing him up, and I'll take *my* talons out," I warned.

He cackled. "Feisty. That's cute. Don't worry, Matteo. I'll take your mind off that. I *do* owe you an apology..."

It was hard to stay annoyed when he started taking off my clothes. He deftly undid my buttons, tossing my newly purchased white shirt aside.

"I just bought that, you know," I pointed out.

"Oh well," he said casually as he undid my belt, clearly not caring. "Guess I'll have to apologize even *harder* then."

The pants disappeared next. I tried to play it cool, but my heart hammered faster than a jackrabbit. Before I had a moment to register my impending nudity, Thystle tucked his thumbs beneath my waistband and slipped my underwear off with an impish smirk.

Nothing remained. I was exposed, completely at Thystle's mercy.

I wasn't used to this. In a past life, I covered up every inch of myself, never showing any part of me—except my eyes. In a twist of fate, I lay now beneath Thystle, naked and vulnerable... except my black eyes. Go figure.

How much did he know? Was he suspicious of my identity, or did he not care? Surely, if he knew the truth, he'd say something...

"Fuck, you're so hot," Thystle murmured. His eyes glinted like amethyst shards. He looked *hungry*. "Let me touch you."

I nodded, too enthralled by him to speak.

Thystle dove in. His hands roamed across my chest and stomach, taking in the sight of my naked body like he was at a museum. It was deeply flattering. I was no stranger to compliments or kind words from fans. I'd been on the receiving end of attention before, but this was different than my experience during years of show business. This felt *real*. Maybe it was because Thystle didn't know who I was. When he touched me, he touched Matteo—not Aquila.

Would he treat me differently if he knew the truth?

Thystle lowered his lips to my waist. His breath ghosted across my skin, making me shiver pleasantly. Joy burst in my chest when he pressed a small kiss to my hip. It was a tiny gesture, but it filled me with happiness. People didn't just kiss random parts of your body unless they were *really* into you.

Thystle's hands snaked down my thighs. He massaged them gently, inching closer to my aching cock. It had been hard for a while. It twitched as Thystle teased it.

Encouraged by my body's reaction, he wrapped his fingers around the base of my cock and shot me a smug grin. I sucked in a sharp breath. The sultry feeling of his hand on my sensitive skin sent electric currents dancing along my spine.

"You like this?" he asked in a low tone.

I nodded again, but that wasn't enough for Thystle this time.

"Tell me, Matteo," he ordered.

Holy fuck, it was hot when he took that dominant tone.

I hadn't spoken because I didn't trust my voice not to crack. "Yes, I like it," I murmured, trying to keep it steady.

Thystle looked amused. "Good, 'cause I'm gonna do a lot more of that."

He squeezed my cock gently, moving his hand upward in a languid motion that shot off fireworks in my skull. I threw my head back against the pillow and hissed in pleasure. My fingers curled against the sheets, bunching them up in my fists, desperate for anything to hold onto. My back arched into Thystle's touch. My body begged for it.

Arousal flared within me, setting my body on fire. Sweat dripped down my temples. I clenched my teeth shut as Thystle worked my cock.

"What, are you worried about the neighbors?" Thystle asked with an edge of irritation. "The rooms are sound-proofed. Let it out."

I hadn't noticed until Thystle pointed it out, but I'd subconsciously held myself back from making noise. I wasn't used to being loud. Not anymore. The last time I'd really belted it out was on stage. It was Aquila who screamed himself raw, not Matteo. Was that why I reined it in?

I stopped biting my lip. Thystle waited, eager to hear my moans and wails. But I hesitated to let loose. For years since the break up, I went out of my way to avoid drawing attention to myself. I didn't want it. I wanted to be plain, to blend into the background. I'd wanted to be Matteo, not Aquila.

Now, it was like I was scared of my own voice, and of the attention it brought upon me. If people knew who I really was, they'd dredge up the past. They'd make me relive the awful moments I tried to forget. I just didn't want conflict anymore.

But Thystle demanded my voice. I didn't want to refuse him.

If anybody knew the truth and accepted me for it, my heart told me it would be Thystle. I wasn't ready to tell him yet, but the least I could do was let him *hear* me.

I dragged myself back to the present. I focused on the sensations coursing through my body. Thystle's hand stroked my sensitive flesh up and down in a steady rhythm. Each brush of his skin against mine zapped my blood. The arousal pooling in the pit of my stomach burned, growing hotter every second.

As Thystle gently squeezed my cock, a moan slipped out of me. It was soft, barely voiced, but it was there.

A feral grin split Thystle's mouth. His eyes flashed with desire.

He liked that.

"Your voice is so hot, Matteo," he murmured. His dragon's growl slipped in, roughing up his tone and revealing his wilder side.

The comment made me flush. I'd heard it before in my past life, but never in this context. This wasn't my singing voice, and I didn't intend to put on a performance. Any sound that came out of me now was raw, organic. It was for Thystle alone.

He rubbed his thumb up along the bottom of my shaft, teasing my head. I shuddered and let out a shaky moan that only encouraged Thystle more. He looked crazed with lust as he leaned in, breathing hard, his lips inches from the tip of my cock.

"Yes, let me hear you," he rasped. He sounded more dragon than human.

Lust sizzled inside my belly. Being wanted like this turned me on fiercely. I wanted to reward Thystle with whatever he desired.

A second later, Thystle wrapped his lips around the head of my cock—and he got exactly what he wanted.

A brazen cry ripped from my throat. The sound of it shocked me. It had been ages since I'd been so loud.

Thystle's mouth around my cock curved into a grin. He loved it. He wanted me to keep going. To speed things along, he sucked my sensitive flesh and earned another moan in return.

"Good," Thystle growled excitedly. "*More.*"

He dove back in, engulfing my cock. The velvety wet heat of Thystle's mouth beckoned me. I couldn't hold back anymore. I bucked my hips instinctively, plunging my cock into that addicting feeling. Thystle easily kept up with my pace. A growl rumbled in his throat as he blew me. The vibration of it made everything ten times hotter.

I felt delirious with pleasure. I let out moans and cries without a care in the world anymore. Sweat drenched my body as the heat of arousal burned within me. The pillow and sheets beneath me were soaked.

And they weren't the only thing, either. My hole twitched, leaking slick. Thystle awakened my omega instincts. If he kept teasing me, I'd lose my fucking mind.

"Fuck me," I blurted out.

Too late. I'd already lost it.

Thystle's eyes widened. His pupils had narrowed into draconic slits, like he was partially transformed. It was beyond sexy.

Unfortunately for my empty hole, Thystle had the mental fortitude to resist.

"We shouldn't. Not yet," he growled, sounding as disappointed as I felt. Then he lifted his hand. "But I *can* do this..."

I gasped as two of his fingers slipped effortlessly into my slick hole. I was so wet that there was barely any friction. Pleasure rocketed up my spine as Thystle angled his fingers, thrusting in and out. As if I wasn't unhinged enough, his mouth captured my cock again.

White hot pleasure crashed into me like a tidal wave. I lost control of myself. My back arched. My hips bucked.

When I came, I let out a loud, ragged scream.

Thystle paused for a split second. He didn't move as my throbbing cock emptied down his throat. A moment later, whatever spell came over him broke. He gulped it all down before popping off with a wet sound.

Meanwhile, I collapsed against the pillow. Stars danced in my vision. I fought for breath until the dizzy spell faded. I couldn't remember the last time I came so hard—or *screamed* so loud.

Suddenly, I sat upright. Thystle hadn't finished yet. I couldn't leave him hanging.

"What about—" I began, then cut myself short.

Thystle breathed hard. His silky hair was damp with sweat, clinging to his forehead. His eyes were glassy with satisfaction. That was when I glanced down to see his flagging cock and a splatter of white droplets against my thighs.

"Did... did you already come?" I asked.

Thystle's cheeks flushed. "Um. Yeah. When you came, you screamed." He paused, as if remembering the sound. "It was really fucking hot."

"Oh," I said, flustered. As far as I knew, nobody had

ever had an orgasm to the sound of my voice before. It was kind of sweet. "Well, sorry I didn't get to be more involved," I added with a chuckle.

"Don't apologize," Thystle grumbled. "I told you, your voice was enough for me."

"I see. Maybe next time I can be more hands-on," I suggested teasingly.

"Then it's a date." He tilted his head, regarding me. "You know, this might be a weird thing to say, but your sexy scream sounded kinda familiar."

My heart lurched.

"Ah," I said, keeping it cool. "Did it?"

"Yeah. It reminded me of Aquila in one of his songs. Remember, that band I was telling you about?"

My mouth fell open. That comment sideswiped me, taking me off guard.

Shit. I knew exactly what song he meant. What should I say? Should I play dumb? Or was it finally time to fess up and tell the truth?

Thystle leapt up as he glanced at the digital clock. "Holy fuck, is that the actual time?"

Saved by the bell.

"Shit," he grumbled. "I don't want to leave, but I have to talk to Jade about the stupid challenges before it's too late to change the next one. You are *not* running another obstacle course or whatever the hell the producers have planned."

"What do you have in mind?"

Thystle scowled while scrambling to put his clothes back on. "I have no clue. Like I said, reality TV isn't my thing."

"What if they were tailored to your interests?" I suggested. "That makes the most sense."

"Yes! That's an amazing idea, Matteo. I'll bring that up to Jade."

Once his clothes were on, he hesitated. He clearly wanted to stay here with me, which felt nice. I wanted him here, too, but his comment about my scream poked my paranoia. I was glad to be off that subject.

"I'll be here if you come back," I said.

Thystle scoffed. "You mean *when* I come back."

My heart skipped a beat.

Just before Thystle left, he glanced at me fondly for a long moment. Then he leaned in, pressed a shy kiss to my cheek, and scampered out of the room.

TWELVE

Thystle

_____

THE LAST THING I wanted to do was abandon Matteo, but I had urgent business to attend to. If I didn't deal with this challenge crap soon, who knew what kind of ridiculous tasks would be sprung on him?

After wrenching myself out of bed and sneaking out of the hotel, I shifted and flew directly to Jade. I suspected he was holed up in his library-turned-office since the beginning of the Games. My hunch was correct. The door was ajar when I reached his library, so I knocked then poked my head in.

"Jade?" I called.

"Thystle. Come in." He greeted me with a smile without lifting his face from the stack of papers. "How go the Games?"

"The Games? Bad. My experience during them overall? Great."

Jade glanced up over the rim of his glasses, giving me a once over. "I'm glad to hear the latter, at least. Why have the Games been bad so far?"

I slumped into the chair across from him. "That's why

I came to talk to you. What's with this obstacle course shit? Who's designing the challenges, a dog trainer?"

Jade paused. He must've realized I was serious because he put down the papers and folded his hands together. "Ah. Gaius told me what happened. Why *did* you miss the first challenge?"

"Does it matter?" I grumbled.

Jade arched a brow. It was such a classic Jade expression. He resembled a stern but fair schoolteacher who was fully aware of my crimes. If he gave someone that look for long enough, they'd confess to anything.

"I overslept, okay?" I admitted, throwing up my hands. "It won't happen again."

"I see." He nodded, still giving me a sly look. "You know, I checked your room, and you weren't there." Dammit.

"I wasn't in my bed," I mumbled. "I was... somewhere else."

The corner of his lips curled into a knowing smirk. "Would that 'somewhere else' have anything to do with why you smell different?"

Heat rushed to my cheeks. I bolted upright in my seat. "I do not!"

Jade thumbed through the papers, unconvinced. "If you say so..."

Why did I even bother trying to fool Jade? He was a living lie detector, like instead of a dragon he was a fucking polygraph shifter.

"Fine. I was with Matteo," I said, crossing my arms. "You squeezed it out of me, you viper."

"I did no such thing," Jade said mildly, knowing exactly what he'd done. "And congratulations. You look happy, Thystle."

The heat in my cheeks intensified. It wasn't often any

of my brothers commented on my visible joy. Not that I was often visibly joyful.

"I am happy," I said under my breath.

Jade flashed a genuine smile. "I'll keep this between us. Duke doesn't need to know."

"Oh, right. The stupid rules." I rolled my eyes. "Thanks, Jade."

He shrugged. "The rules are for good TV, not for real relationships. At the end of the day, it's your happiness that matters. That's the whole point of the Games."

As much as my brothers got on my nerves, I didn't want to be the reason they missed a chance to find love.

"Yeah, but if Duke finds out and gets pissed, he might not want to produce any more seasons," I pointed out. "I don't want anyone to get screwed because of me."

Jade wasn't concerned. "Duke gets paid handsomely. It's enough incentive to produce seasons of this show for the rest of his life. He may be a grouch, but he's no fool. Don't worry, Thystle."

I nodded slowly. "So... it's okay that I like Matteo?"

"Why wouldn't it be?"

"Because the Games have barely started, and I'm head over heels for him. It's not really fair to everyone else."

"Did Crimson worry when he fell in love with Taylor?" Jade countered.

"I dunno. I guess not. I still haven't watched the show," I admitted.

Jade's brows raised. "You haven't?"

"Geez, was I supposed to? I want to watch it, I've just... been busy."

Jade smirked. "I can imagine."

I flushed, wanting to change the subject since I didn't want Jade thinking about my sex life. "Let's get back on topic. The challenges, remember?"

Jade leaned forward. "All right. What about them?"

"They suck," I said bluntly. "No more obstacle courses, or other shit like that."

Jade pulled out a pen and crossed off some text on a piece of paper. "Noted. What would you prefer?"

I shifted my weight in my seat. I didn't exactly have a plan when I stormed up to Jade's office. Since I'd already fallen for Matteo, none of the other contestants stood a chance. How could I tailor the challenges in his favor without being too obvious about it? Not that I cared that much. At the end of the day, Matteo would *always* be my choice.

I recalled our conversation. An idea sparked in my mind.

"If the challenges are supposed to figure out who my fated mate is, shouldn't they be about my interests?" I asked.

Jade hummed in affirmation. "Yes, that's a good idea. Any suggestions?"

I mulled it over. "What about... a quiz? The second challenge could test what the contestants know about me. I mean, if they want to be my mate, they should know a thing or two about the bachelor, right?"

Jade's pen flew across the paper. "Excellent. Anything else?"

I wracked my brain, but my mind-blowing afternoon with Matteo had turned it to mush. "You put me on the spot here... Can you give me time to think about it?"

"I can spare a day or two, but not much more. We need time to prepare the set and make arrangements," Jade said.

"That's fair. I'll think of something," I promised. "Thanks, Jade."

"Of course. I want the Games to be as rewarding for you as they were for Crimson."

Was that a hint of envy in Jade's voice? I wondered if he looked forward to his turn. Jade never made a fuss about finding his fated mate, but he was an alpha dragon all the same. It was instinct. We couldn't stave it off.

Speaking of which, my instincts were pissed at me for leaving Matteo alone in his hotel room. There was nothing I could do about it, though. My best option was to head home and finally watch the first season of the Dragonfate Games, just like I promised.

My hopes of a relaxing night watching Matteo on TV were dashed as soon as I opened my bedroom door. The smell of popcorn wafted from inside. A pair of uninvited guests sat on the floor, leaning against my bed and staring at my laptop screen.

"What the hell are you two doing in my room?" I grouched at the twins.

"Oops. Busted," Saffron said. He made no attempt to move except to toss another piece of popcorn in his mouth.

"Oh, hey, Thystle," Aurum said without wrenching his gaze off the screen. "Come on, we just started episode three. This is a juicy one."

If I hadn't let off so much steam with Matteo, I might've shifted and clawed their ears off. Because I had, the twins' unwanted presence only mildly infuriated me.

"Why are you even in here? And what are you watching?" I demanded.

"Dragonfate Games season one," they said in unison.

I instantly forgot about my anger. I leapt onto the bed and stared at the laptop screen, watching closely for any sign of Matteo.

"Where is he?" I blurted.

"Who?" Saffron asked curiously.

I blushed. I'd forgotten that only Jade knew. "Nothing, never mind."

Aurum snorted. "You can't just say that and then pretend it's not important."

"Shut up."

Saffron wasn't willing to let it go either. He turned around, narrowing his eyes at me. "Who's *he?* I wanna know."

"Nobody," I insisted. "Pass the popcorn."

Saffron scrutinized me, as if I'd admit the truth if he stared long enough, but eventually he gave up and thrust the bowl in my hands.

I was halfway to shoving a handful of popcorn in my mouth when the screen panned to a wide shot of the forest cliffs. Was this one of the challenges? I paused, my mouth hanging open as the shot changed. All the omega contestants waited in animal form at the starting line.

"What is this?" I asked.

"Race to the top," Aurum said, sounding bored. "Whoever's first wins, except not really, 'cause Crimson chooses an actual winner regardless of who was first."

Guilt wormed in my belly. That wasn't what happened today. Since I was absent, Gaius felt forced to choose a winner based on points... and that was Talon. I tried not to feel too bad about it. After all, Matteo's jealousy about it ended up in a round of hot sex.

As Gaius said go, all the omegas took off. I held my breath as I searched for a golden eagle. My heart stumbled over itself when I saw him.

There!

Matteo, in all his winged glory, soared to the top of the cliff without a problem. This challenge was incredibly easy for him. For all intents and purposes, *he* should've been the

106

clear winner—but I sure as hell was glad he wasn't. Thinking about Crimson picking Matteo as his date made my blood boil. Matteo was *mine*.

But Crimson wasn't after anybody's mate but his own, and that was Taylor. The camera spent most of its time zoomed in on him and his selfless rescue effort. Seeing Taylor save Muzo from the boulder was nice and all, but I wished the camera would pan back to Matteo, who perched patiently at the top of the cliff.

After what felt like a century, the shot changed to the clifftop where all the winning omegas were gathered. I leaned in, eyes wide and heart racing as I stared at Matteo.

"Is *that* who you're into?" Saffron asked, close to my face.

I jolted. Since when had Saffron been watching me so closely? Creep.

"What? No," I blurted.

He flashed a rascally grin. "Don't bother. You can't fool me. I see that sentimental look in your eyes."

Aurum glanced over. "What are you talking about? He looks the same as always."

"He literally doesn't," Saffron argued.

"He literally does."

Saffron made a face like his twin was delusional. "Can't you see it?"

Aurum scoffed. "See what? His smudged eyeliner?"

Mercury must've been in retrograde if the twins disagreed this much about something.

"My eyeliner is *not* smudged," I grouched. "Anyway, pipe down, I'm trying to watch the show."

Saffron ignored me, frowning at Aurum. "Do you seriously not notice that Thystle's brain is scrambled?"

I huffed. "My brain is not—"

Aurum cut me off. "No? Are you high or something? I can't believe you'd do that without me..."

"I'm *not* high. Look at him," Saffron urged, gesturing at me. "He has the same dopey expression he wore all the time as a teenager, when he was obsessed with that singer."

I couldn't even be annoyed at their comments. I was too surprised that the twins were in the middle of a real argument. I'd never seen them at odds like this before.

Aurum gave me a half-hearted look before shrugging. "Nope. Don't see it. Anyway, who cares?"

"I do!" Saffron insisted. "Thystle's obviously in love!"

"So what?"

Saffron and I both let out a derisive scoff—which shocked me. Saffron *never* agreed with me over his twin. This Twilight Zone shit was starting to freak me out.

"I care that our brother's in love, and so should you. One of these days, it's gonna be *our* turn to find our fated mates," Saffron explained.

Aurum stared at his twin with a blank face. Eventually, he sighed and ate another handful of popcorn. "Great," he snarked. "Can't wait for that."

Saffron and I exchanged a what-the-fuck-is-happening glance. This was beyond my pay grade. Whatever Aurum's attitude problem was, Saffron would figure it out. I hoped.

But I forgot all about my brothers' issues as the screen showed Matteo's face.

I rushed forward and slammed my finger onto the pause button, forcing the screen to linger on him. Heart racing, my eyes glued to the laptop, I forgot how to breathe. Fuck, he was drop-dead gorgeous.

His eyes were the same warm shade of amber brown, but this time, they weren't obscured. I witnessed them in their full glory.

A creeping recognition came to me. I *knew* those eyes. They were deeply familiar to me in a way I couldn't place.

I scrutinized them, leaning in as close as I could. They belonged to Matteo, sans the obvious purple swelling. But there was something else I couldn't put my finger on...

"There it is again," Saffron said knowingly.

"What?" Aurum grumbled.

"See that face Thystle's making? Same one he made for *that* guy. He's in love."

From the corner of my eye, I saw Saffron gesturing at my old Aquila poster. Instinctively, I turned to look at him, my masked crush of ten long years. My jaw dropped as I stared at the poster, dumbfounded.

Matteo had Aquila's eyes. The exact same ones.

Without a word, I slowly rose from the bed and ran off into the hall towards Jade's library. The whole time I kept remembering Matteo's scream in bed. I *knew* it sounded familiar. It was Aquila's raw, primal scream, the one that chilled me to my core every time I listened to his music.

When I appeared in Jade's doorway again in a huff, he looked up from his strewn papers in surprise.

"Thystle," he said. "What's wrong?"

I was convinced I already knew the answer, but I needed outside confirmation.

"What's the Latin name for golden eagles?" I demanded.

Jade blinked. "*Aquila chrysaetos.* Why do you ask?"

THIRTEEN

Matteo

I FELL ASLEEP WAITING for Thystle's return. It was late by the time he left, and I was exhausted from our tryst, so I was content to cozy up in the bed that still smelled like him.

The next morning, I showered thoroughly—my friends were canine and feline shifters with keener senses of smell than mine, and I didn't want to tip them off—then ambled down to the lobby. The crowd had noticeably thinned. I suspected many of them stayed up too late partying and missed their morning alarms.

But for better or for worse, the ones who were serious about the Dragonfate Games were present. My friends were all bright-eyed and ready to face the next challenge. Poppy floated by Muzo's side as the jackal shifter stretched his gangly limbs. Alaric took a tiny sip of complimentary coffee, though the milky concoction in his cup was more cream than coffee at this point.

Talon mingled on the other side of the lobby. I prayed he didn't notice me. I didn't care for our shared kinship as eagles, or his gloating. If he bragged to my face, I might passive-aggressively let it slip that I blew my load down Thystle's throat last night.

"If you're going to dislike somebody, you should be subtle about it," Alaric remarked under his breath.

I smirked. "Coming from you, Alaric? Your disdain for Taylor in season one was as subtle as a bomb."

He sniffed. "Exactly. I learned my lesson. If you want everyone to know you hate Talon, you should stop glaring at him from across the room."

"I don't *hate* him. I just don't care for him."

"Sure. Do pigs fly, too?"

Muzo butted in. "They can, if you put a pig shifter on a plane!"

Alaric let out a theatrical sigh. "Why do I even bother?"

"The concept of a flying pig is scary," Poppy murmured, rubbing his arm. "That boar we hunted in season one was terrifying enough..."

"Oh, for gods' sake," Alaric snapped. "You're a wolf. Don't you have any pride?"

Poppy meekly disappeared behind Muzo's shoulder, avoiding the question.

"Hey, pride doesn't mean squat if you're dead," Muzo pointed out. "Don't try to tell me that boar didn't freak you out, too, Alaric. All your fur went *poof* during that hunt."

Alaric narrowed his eyes. "That was a different situation."

It was too early in the morning for this tension. I swooped into the conversation to save all three of them.

"Thystle spoke to me about the challenges," I said. "There shouldn't be any dangerous ones from now on." Alaric's pencil-thin brow arched sharply. "When did he speak to you? Nobody saw him yesterday."

Shit. In my effort to dissolve the conflict, I'd dug myself

into a hole.

"After the challenge ended, we went back to our rooms. So, where were *you*?" Alaric accused.

His odd eyes sharpened into daggers of blue and green. I understood now why Taylor often clashed with him. Being on the receiving end of Alaric's ire wasn't pleasant. But I wasn't as eager to fight back as Taylor. I avoided conflict between friends, but more than anything, I loathed being the source of it. I'd had enough of that for one lifetime.

My instinct to keep the peace warred with my desire to keep my rendezvous with Thystle a secret. Would Alaric understand if I told him the truth—or would he turn on me, just like all the others?

"Why, he was with me!" Talon declared. The other eagle shifter appeared out of nowhere, throwing a friendly arm around me and flashing Alaric a million-dollar grin.

Both of Alaric's brows disappeared beneath his bangs. "He was?"

I swallowed a groan. What the hell was Talon doing? If he was trying to save me, his timing was abysmal. Barely five minutes had passed since I'd spoken to Alaric about my dislike of the man.

"Of course. After the challenge, Thystle pulled us feathered folk aside for a little chat," Talon proclaimed, then winked. "Consider it a little after party between the winner and the runner up."

Alaric glanced back and forth at the two of us, unsure of who to believe. I didn't blame him. I thought I was a decent liar, but Talon was like a boasting politician. If I shattered Talon's lie, we'd both look bad. Maybe I owed it to Talon to play along. I didn't know why he did it, but he *did* save me from an uncomfortable conversation.

"That's right," I said. It came easily because it wasn't a

total lie—I *had* spoken to Thystle after the challenge, just under different circumstances than Talon's story.

"I see," Alaric replied, his expression unreadable.

Talon clicked his tongue. "Ah! I forgot my drink by the table. Come on, Matteo."

There was no room in his statement for disagreement. I waved a quick goodbye to my friends before Talon whisked me to the opposite end of the lobby and hid us behind a pillar. There was no drink on any table.

"So, my feathered companion, let's trade," Talon began, still wearing that blindingly white grin. "I saved you from a sticky situation. Now you owe me."

Of course there was a catch. Not that I was surprised.

"What do you want?" I asked.

"Information. What did Thystle tell you about the next challenges?"

I shrugged. "If you want specifics, you're out of luck. All I know is that he wants them tailored towards his interests."

Talon nodded. "Those bands he likes."

I bristled. How did he know that?

Before I could ask, Talon grinned proudly. "I dug around before the Games began. A pair of guys I met knew a surprising amount about Thystle."

A pair of guys with a lot of info? Did he mean the twins?

"What did they say?" I asked.

Talon smirked. "I don't know if I should share. You *are* competition, after all."

I stifled the urge to scoff. There was no competition anymore—but I was the only omega who knew that. I kept my relationship with Thystle to myself. For Talon, ignorance was bliss.

"Fair enough," I said.

The fact that I was unbothered bothered Talon. A tick appeared in his previously brilliant smile.

"Well, since you played along with me earlier, I guess I can spill a bit of info," Talon conceded. He lowered his voice. "Rumor has it Thystle is hot for a certain music celebrity." His mouth split in a scheming grin. "And he's here among us."

I blinked, taken aback, but kept my expression neutral. Talon spoke as if he knew a lot... but how much did he actually know? He couldn't suspect me of being that particular celebrity—he had no proof. Besides, if he *did* suspect me, he wouldn't declare it to my face.

Then who the hell was he talking about?

"Hello, contestants!" Gaius greeted over the noisy lobby.

"Time's up. Good luck on the next challenge," Talon murmured before melting into the crowd.

Somehow, I doubted he meant that.

"It's a new day, and that means a new challenge!" Gaius announced. "Follow me outside."

As everyone left the lobby, we saw a new development on the beachfront. A flashy stage was set up with a podium and a throne-like chair. Before the stage were rows of chairs. It looked like a game show set. It never failed to surprise me how quickly the staff set up challenges.

"Omega contestants, please take your seats," Gaius said, gesturing to the chairs.

I sat near the front next to Muzo, Poppy and Alaric. For whatever reason, Talon took the seat next to me. I was grateful that Gaius hopped on stage to begin his host spiel so I didn't have to talk awkwardly with anybody.

"Today's challenge is a very exciting one," Gaius assured as he strode across the stage. "For the first time ever on the Dragonfate Games, we're hosting a quiz show!

What's the topic, you might ask? Why, it's our one and only smoldering alpha dragon bachelor—it's Thystle!"

My heart soared as Thystle appeared from behind the back curtain and joined Gaius on stage. I couldn't stop myself from sitting up sharply and leaning forward in my seat. Thankfully, everybody else seemed too enthralled with Thystle's first challenge appearance to notice. A few people cheered and whooped, but Thystle paid them no mind.

He was staring right into my eyes.

Everyone beside me turned to look. Heat bloomed in my cheeks—and to my embarrassment, between my thighs as well.

So much for my cover.

Thystle blinked hard, then wrenched his gaze away from me. I let out a silent breath of relief. With Thystle's attention on Gaius, nobody commented on the random staring contest between us.

Gaius patted Thystle's back like he was tapping the hood of a prized car. "That's right! Today's challenge is all about Thystle. What do you know? What *don't* you know? And will it be enough to win the dragon's heart today?"

I tamped down a flicker of irritation at that comment. I knew Gaius played up the drama for the cameras, and hell, he didn't even *know* about my relationship with Thystle.

How would I describe our relationship, anyway? I didn't have the words for it. Calling it a crush felt pale and weak, and calling it a one-night stand was too cheap. Whatever I felt for Thystle was beyond comparison.

My heart clenched. Had I fallen in love with Thystle?

Gaius summoned everyone's attention. "One at a time, our omega contestants will take the stand. I'll ask questions about our bachelor. Each correct answer yields a point, and gets you closer to the winner's circle!"

Alaric thrust his hand up.

"Yes?" Gaius said.

"What does that mean?" Alaric asked. "Will the one with the most points automatically be deemed the winner, like in the first challenge? Or is this like the first season, where the bachelor gets the final say?"

Thystle spoke up before Gaius could respond. "I choose."

Talon sniffed, squaring his shoulders. "What's the reward for this challenge? I didn't get anything last time."

"You got an after party with Thystle and Matteo," Alaric pointed out.

Thystle looked confused. He didn't know what Alaric was talking about, since Talon had made that up.

"I'm sorry for not being there for the first challenge. I'll make it up to the winner later," Thystle said, giving Talon a quick glance. His tone made it obvious that was a hassle he didn't want to deal with.

Talon didn't seem to notice. For him, any attention was good. He sat up straighter with a smug grin, eager for his reward. I resisted the urge to roll my eyes. Whatever he thought would happen between him and Thystle was a fantasy.

There was no mistaking the predatory glint in Thystle's eyes when he looked my way. It was enough to make me hard, sitting there in the crowd. I shifted my legs so it wasn't obvious.

"Alaric makes a good point," Gaius said, nodding. "What's a challenge without a prize? For today's challenge, the prize is... a moonlit beach date with Thystle!"

Excited murmurs sprang up among the crowd.

I leaned closer to the edge of my seat. This time, I wasn't going to let Talon or anyone else steal it from me. That date was *mine*.

FOURTEEN

Thystle

IT TOOK every last atom of my willpower not to stare at Matteo. It was like trying to ignore the booming foghorn and blaring brightness of a lighthouse while standing right next to it. Almost fucking impossible.

I had half a mind to call this whole thing off, declare the Games over, and jump Matteo's bones right in the middle of everybody. But though that'd make great TV, it wasn't a great look for us dragons. The world only just found out we still existed at all. Making us all look like horny devils on national TV wasn't the play here. I had to bite my lip and bide my time until this stupid challenge was over. Then I'd take him home and fuck his brains out all night long.

He was Aquila. I was positive of that now. He stared me in the face this whole time, yet a couple black eyes had obscured the truth. Not anymore. I knew that sexy scream and those golden-brown eyes off by heart.

You can't run from me, Matteo.

"...the first round! Please welcome to the stage... Poppy Faolan!"

Gaius's announcer voice yanked me from my daze.

Ugh, of all the times to be thrust in front of a crowd and camera crew. All I wanted was to pin Matteo to the ground and claim him, but I had to get through this shit first.

I plastered a smile onto my face. It edged closer to being genuine when I saw the meek omega climb on stage. His blond hair was so pale, it matched the coat of his Arctic wolf form. I felt bad for Poppy. He looked like he wanted to be on stage just as much as I did—which was to say, not at all.

"H-hello," he said on the opposite edge of the stage.

"Hi there," I replied.

Gaius guided Poppy to the podium, since the omega looked glued to the floorboards in fear, then gave him a reassuring pat.

"Don't be nervous. This is a great opportunity to test your knowledge," Gaius said to Poppy, then grabbed the mic. "All right! First question. I'll throw you a bone, kiddo. What color is Thystle's dragon form?"

Poppy trembled. The poor guy looked like he was about to faint.

"Um... uh," he whispered.

"Don't forget the microphone," Gaius reminded him with a smile.

Poppy instantly forgot about the microphone. "Erm, ah... it's... purple?"

Gaius gave a slight nod, trying to encourage him. "Gotta be more specific. What shade of purple?"

Poppy sweated bullets. His gaze flickered from me to Gaius, to the onlookers, to the cameras. He swayed on his feet. "V...violet?"

Oh, poor sweet Poppy. He'd mixed me up with my freak brother. If he couldn't even handle being on stage, he wouldn't last a second with Viol.

I nudged Gaius with my elbow and mumbled, "This is torture. Let him go."

"Time's up, Poppy! That was a good effort, we'll give you half a point for that," Gaius said, leading Poppy off stage with a smile. "Up next, we have Muzo Zavala!"

I resisted the urge to groan. How many times did I have to do this? I risked a glance to the front row. Matteo wasn't too far off. Only a couple more contestants until it was his turn. Out of everybody, he knew me best. He'd win for sure. Then we'd put this challenge to rest and get down to business. As in, me plowing him into next Tuesday.

Unlike Poppy, Muzo basked in the attention. He pranced onto the stage and took the podium. "Yay, I love game shows!"

He was cute, but so not my type. None of these omegas were my type except one. And the longer I spent apart from him, the more I wanted to rip my hair out.

"Muzo! Here's your first question," Gaius began, clearing his throat. "What is Thystle's age?"

Muzo blinked rapidly. "Uh..."

I practically heard the static noise in his brain. How was he supposed to know? I'd barely spoken to him.

"Can I get a hint?" Muzo asked with a sheepish grin.

Gaius nodded, checking his cue cards. "Sure. Thystle is six years *younger* than his favorite celebrity. You have thirty seconds to respond."

That comment stunned me. Jade really did his home-work. He must've stayed up all night writing the questions after I asked him for help.

The clue did nothing to help Muzo, who had no idea. But I caught Matteo's expression changing from the corner of my eye. Of course *he* knew the answer. I couldn't stifle a smirk. As each second crept by, I grew more eager for him to take the stage.

Gaius imitated a buzzer noise. "Sorry, Muzo, time's up."

"Aw, man," Muzo grumbled as he moped down to the front row.

"Next up!" Gaius swept his arm. "Alaric St. Clair!"

I steeled myself. I'd heard all about the haughty cat shifter from Taylor's stories. Alaric had been determined to beat Taylor and earn his place as Crimson's mate, which obviously didn't happen. Was he just as tenacious and keen to sink his claws into me?

The white-haired twink sauntered to the podium. There was no fear in his eyes like Poppy, and no silly vibe like Muzo. But Alaric's gaze was only hard, not predatory. Did he sense I wasn't interested?

Gaius held the mic to his mouth as he read off the card. "Alaric, here's your first question. What is Thystle's color as a dragon?"

Alaric's odd eyes flashed. "Amethyst. Next question."

The crowd rustled in excitement. That was the first correct answer, but it was an easy one. I made no effort to hide that fact.

Gaius was all worked up. "We got a hot one, folks! One point for you, Alaric. Can you win another?"

"I don't know, can I?" he asked sarcastically. He shot me a dry, unimpressed look, as if this whole thing was rigged.

In a way, it was. I felt sorry for him. Alaric had been through this once before with Crimson, and now with me. It couldn't be easy for an omega craving love to be rejected twice in a row. Hell, I hadn't even formally rejected him yet, but Alaric wasn't stupid. He'd already figured out I had no desire to be with him. The Dragonfate Games seriously needed to start offering consolation prizes.

Gaius was immune to the negativity brewing on stage.

He was as upbeat as ever. "That's up to you, my friend. Here's your second question. Maybe you can answer one from earlier. So, I'll ask again: what does Thystle hoard?"

I watched Alaric, curious to hear his response. He was shrewd, sure, but we'd barely spoken. If he knew, he would've found out through a third party.

But Alaric shook his head. "Eyeliner?"

Gaius made another buzzer sound. "Sorry, Alaric, your reign ends here."

Huffing, Alaric trudged off stage. I didn't know if he knew the answer and blew it on purpose as a 'fuck you' to the whole charade, or if he genuinely had no clue, but I felt bad for dragging him into this either way.

As I watched him sit next to Matteo, my heart skipped a beat. He was next.

It was him. Only him. He'd win this challenge, and the entire Games. I knew that because he'd already won my heart.

My eyes caught Matteo's. Sparks exploded in my chest. Instinctively, I knew he felt the same way. An invisible magnetic bond spanned between us, linking us together with cosmic force. I gripped the arms of the throne hard, forcing myself to stay seated until Matteo made it to the stage. Pinning him to the stage on TV was probably a no-no.

But as Matteo rose from his seat, Talon's arm thrust out in front of him. The other man stood confidently and raised a hand.

"I have a proposal," Talon announced.

My heart sank. What the fuck was he prattling about? I wanted Matteo *now*, dammit.

I didn't bother wiping the petulant scowl off my face as Gaius shot me a questioning look. Seeing he wasn't getting any help out of me, Gaius faced Talon with a polite smile.

"Sure. Let's hear it," he said.

Talon mirrored Gaius's flashy grin with his own. "As the winner of the first challenge, wouldn't it make sense for me to be allowed to cut the line? That way, my accomplishment earns a real benefit in the Games."

My heart plummeted further, dropping like an anchor to the ocean floor. I tried to telepathically beam the word 'NO' into Gaius's brain, but there was no light at the end of the tunnel. In the battle between two charismatic loud-mouths, Talon's wiles had won this battle. Gaius couldn't refuse him without making the Games seem ultra rigged, which Alaric had alluded to moments ago—and if the Games were *too* rigged, future applicants may not be interested.

"Fair enough," Gaius conceded. "Come on up."

I noted with amusement that Gaius didn't mention his name at all. The gryphon clearly didn't like Talon showing him up like that. I took solace in the fact that we were on the same page about Talon being a smarmy smart ass.

Talon strode up to the podium. He oozed confidence in a way that made me want to gag. It wasn't the quiet, calm confidence that Matteo had. Talon's aura throbbed like a migraine-inducing nightclub, loud and over the top. He looked like he wanted to induct me into a pyramid scheme.

"Hello, Thystle," Talon greeted.

I hated this.

"Hi." I couldn't force a smile, but hey, I got the word out in one piece.

Talon didn't seem to notice my sinister mood, but Gaius did. He distracted the crowd by dramatically sweeping across the stage, putting his showmanship on blast.

"What a shocking new development!" Gaius

announced. "Will our contestant earn points, or will he crash and burn? Let's find out."

The corner of my mouth tweaked into a smirk. Damn, Gaius was savage when he wanted to be. I recognized he was throwing shade at Talon, but his cheerful host voice was so charismatic and mesmerizing that I doubted anybody in the crowd thought anything of it.

"I'm ready," Talon replied, his hands coolly tucked into his pockets.

I ignored him. My gaze connected with Matteo's in the front row.

He was *fuming*.

I'd never seen him look so pissed. He radiated fury, his eyes diamond-hard and narrowed into daggers. Fuck, that turned me on.

I willed Gaius to lob impossible questions at Talon so we could get this shit over with already. If I didn't plunge my dick into Matteo soon, I'd explode.

"Let's start with a question everyone else has failed," Gaius began. "Talon, what does Thystle h—"

Talon cut him off with an arrogant grin. "He hoards music."

Gaius's grip on the cue cards tightened ever so slightly.

Oh, yeah. Gaius was pissed, too.

I withheld a snort of laughter. It took a *lot* to anger Gaius. He was the definition of laid back. Hell, when he wasn't working, the guy wore Hawaiian shirts and drank margaritas on the beach all day. Something about Talon must've rubbed his feathers the wrong way. The feeling was mutual among his fellow winged shifters. Me, Gaius, and Matteo all disliked the guy.

Gaius let out a tilted laugh. "Eager to spit out that answer, eh?"

That earned a chuckle from the audience. They

thought Gaius was being playful, which he was, but I knew him well enough to recognize the irritation in his voice.

"Well, you're in luck because that *was* going to be my question. Wait 'til I get the next one out, all right?" Talon nodded. "Yes, I will."

Gaius whipped out the next cue card. "Here's your second, another one that was previously answered wrong. How old is Thystle?"

I'd never spoken to Talon about my age, but it wasn't exactly a secret. He could've asked around for it. Shit.

My dread came to fruition when Talon smiled and said, "He's 27."

Gaius returned a thin smile. "Correct! That's two for two so far."

I withheld a groan as I sank in the throne. I wished a meteor would drop on the stage. Anything to escape this miserable situation.

I glanced over at Matteo, no longer caring if anybody noticed. He sat stiffly in his chair, and his hands balled up into fists on his knees. He was suffering through this just as much as I was. If only I could sit next to him and hold his hand, reassuring him everything would be okay.

Unfortunately, Talon had gotten every question right so far. I prayed Gaius would trip him up and throw an impossible question his way.

Gaius squinted at the next cue card, then pocketed the whole stack. I raised a brow, sitting upright. What was he doing?

"Okay, Talon. Question number three," Gaius said. "What is Thystle's all-time favorite band?"

My heart fluttered as Matteo's back went ramrod straight. *He* knew this.

Holy fucking Drake, I wished it was him on stage instead of Talon.

Instead of crumpling under pressure like I hoped would happen, Talon flashed a slow, confident grin.

"That would be TalonStorm, of course," he stated.

My heart turned to lead and sank. How did he know that? And why did he look so fucking smug about it? I glanced sidelong at Matteo. He froze like he stopped breathing. His eyes were wide, staring at Talon. Then he caught my eye and hope flickered in my chest. There was something conspiratorial swirling in them, a whispered secret we shared that took the edge off my despair.

I knew Matteo's true identity.

Did *he* know I knew?

The crowd murmured again, wowed by Talon's knowledge.

Gaius cleared his throat, ready to move on. "You're three for three so far."

Talon smirked. "Is there a limit to the number of points I can win?"

I resisted the urge to gag. His cheeky remarks came across as arrogant rather than confident. He lacked a certain warmth and star quality that Gaius had.

"Sky's the limit," Gaius remarked, shooting me a glance.

Help, I wanted to mouth. But since this was all on tape, I refrained.

"Go on," Talon urged. "I'm ready for the next question."

Before Gaius could respond, I stood up from the throne. "I'll ask it," I announced.

That got everyone's attention. But among the sea of shocked faces, my focus was on Matteo. His brown eyes glinted, as enraptured with me as I was with him. I could tell by the barely hidden desire in his gaze that he desperately wanted to be on stage beside me.

As a dragon, I was impatient as fuck. Enough was enough. It was time to shut this down.

I took the microphone from Gaius, who was relieved yet curious at my sudden interruption. Standing on the opposite end of the stage from Talon, I raised the mic to my lips.

"What's the name of TalonStorm's debut album?" I asked.

The crowd went silent, eagerly watching Talon for his response.

Talon broke out into a grin. "*Wings of the Sun.*"

I stilled. How did he know? Was he a fan? If so, why hadn't he brought it up until now? It didn't sit right with me.

Before I could ask the next question, Talon chuckled. "I bet you're wondering how I know that."

Something was fishy.

"Tell me," I said.

"You know what kind of shifter I am, don't you?" he shot back.

Get to the freaking point already, I thought.

"A Steller's sea eagle, right?" I replied.

"That's right. Also known as..." He paused for effect. "*Aquila pelagica.*"

The first part of his name rang a bell, but it didn't affect my opinion of him. Other eagles shared that taxonomy. I *knew* he wasn't Aquila.

"And?" I asked.

Talon wasn't deterred by my questioning. It almost seemed to fuel his arrogant confidence. "And I believe you've been a fan of mine for quite a while."

My brows jumped up. "Have I?"

He flipped his perfectly styled hair back and grinned

an unnaturally white smile. "Does the name Aquila ring a bell?"

I stared at him, dumbstruck by the gall of this guy. Was he seriously trying to imply he was Aquila, lead singer of TalonStorm? I choked out a laugh, then tried to disguise it as a coughing fit. From the corner of my eye, I saw a wisp of amusement stirring on Matteo's lips.

Talon's face finally fell. That clearly wasn't the reaction he expected.

"Sorry," I said, clearing my throat. "I must've swallowed a bug."

Talon sniffed. He squared his shoulders, standing up straighter. I didn't know if he was trying to save face, or if he believed his own wild story. "What do you think, Thystle?" he asked, mouth curving into a smirk again. "Want to ask the next question? Or should we call the challenge here?"

Oh, brother.

"Sure, Talon," I said. "Ready for the next question?"

"Shoot."

From the corner of my eye, I saw Matteo staring at me intently. I wondered if he was enjoying this charade, too.

"Here goes," I said chipperly. "Which ass cheek is my birthmark on?"

Talon paled, his jaw going slack.

It was over now.

Talon gulped. "Your... left."

Now it was my turn to feel smug. "Wrong. I don't have a birthmark on my ass cheek. You can take a seat."

FIFTEEN

Matteo

———————

MY INITIAL DREAD at Talon taking my place on stage evaporated the second he started making a fool of himself. By the end of his run, I was biting my lip so I didn't wheeze with laughter. Though, if it were me answering that last question, I would've gotten hard remembering the sight of Thystle's bare ass the night before. Maybe it was a good thing I was hidden among the crowd for that one.

As Talon trudged back to his seat, I tried to keep the shit-eating grin off my face. No need to rub salt in his wounds—even if he *did* try to commit identity theft in front of everybody.

Gaius swept across the stage and gestured to me. "All right, next contestant, please! Matteo, you're up!" My heart tripped over itself as I stood. Muzo put his thumbs up, Poppy smiled, and Alaric gave me a knowing nod. Their encouragement overrode the nasty glare I felt on the back of my head, no doubt coming from Talon.

But I forgot all about him as I reached the top of the stairs. As my gaze met Thystle's, warmth bloomed in my body, seeping through my limbs. There was something different in his eyes. A sharp, predatory knowing, like he'd stabbed his sword into the truth of who I was. My heart fluttered with a twisted mix of anxiety and relief. How much did Thystle know? How did he feel about it? Was he upset I hadn't confessed earlier?

Meeting his hot gaze, I doubted that. They blazed with desire, the kind that would never be satisfied. A shiver ran down my spine. To be wanted by a dragon was thrilling. I felt like a butterfly pinned to a board, stared at adoringly by a collector for all time.

Biting down the urge to run to Thystle, I stepped behind the podium. Thystle's mouth curved into a grin across from me. He stood in front of the throne, still holding the mic.

Gaius let out a playful laugh and stepped aside. "Well, it looks like I've been usurped as the host of this challenge, so take it away, Thystle. These questions are about *you*, after all."

Thystle nodded at his friend. "Thanks, Gaius." Then his glittering amethyst eyes stabbed into me like fishhooks. "Matteo. First question."

I shuddered at the sultry way he said my name.

"How long is the first track on *Wings of the Sun*?" Thystle asked, staring directly at me.

I was keenly aware of the crowd's gaze. Did they expect me to fail this niche question, or did they think I'd nail it like Talon did the first few times?

But the crowd didn't know what Thystle did—that *I* was Aquila. I saw it in the way his hungry alpha gaze blazed with feral *want*, yet also shone with the brilliance of a die-hard fan. The only thing stopping Thystle from jumping me was the cameras. Stupid reality TV.

I nodded at Thystle across the stage. "Five minutes even."

He sucked in a breath, his fingers curling tighter around the mic. "Correct," he murmured.

"One point for Matteo!" Gaius announced. "Wow, even I didn't know the answer to that one."

The crowd cheered, impressed by my arcane knowledge. A bittersweet feeling swirled in my gut. It had been so long since I was on stage with people cheering for me, and now it was happening again under such strange circumstances.

Thystle's frame tensed in excitement, like he wanted to pounce on me. "Next question," he said rapidly, as if out of breath. "How many albums did TalonStorm put out?"

"Including EPs?" I asked.

His eyes flashed. "Obviously."

"Four."

He inhaled a ragged breath and licked his lips. "Correct."

The crowd exploded into shock and awe.

"That's two points for Matteo!" Gaius announced. "And wow, what points they are. Who knew they had so much in common?"

That sounded like a pointed jab at Talon, but being on stage with Thystle made me forget all my disdain for him. Right now, it was just the two of us—the way it should've been.

"On which track is Aquila's longest vocal solo?" Thystle asked.

A shiver jolted down my spine. I knew exactly which track Thystle referenced—the one with my long, raw scream. The same one he recognized in bed. It'd been ages since I sang that song, but Thystle had gotten a private taste of it.

He was such an ass for bringing that up in front of all these people. A breathy laugh came out of me.

"*Destiny Rises,*" I replied.

Thystle didn't blink. His stare burned a hole into me. "Correct."

Gaius laughed. "Wow. You're on a roll, Matteo! Three for three so far."

Thystle didn't hesitate to launch into the next one. "Who are the other two band members of TalonStorm?"

I exhaled through my nose. That struck a sore spot, but I didn't dwell on it like I usually would. The high of being on stage and the pleasure of lobbying back and forth with Thystle swamped any anxieties swimming in my gut.

"Vani and Keaux," I said, their faces flashing in my mind.

"Correct."

Gaius shrugged and mimed tossing his cue cards over his shoulder, causing the crowd to laugh.

"In which city was TalonStorm's last concert supposed to take place in?" Thystle asked.

The last concert before the band broke up. It must've been a sore spot for Thystle.

"Glazeby," I recalled, remembering it well. I looked forward to its calm energy compared to some of the heavy nightlife in other tours.

A slow grin spread over Thystle's face. "You got it."

"Five correct answers!" Gaius exclaimed. His positive attitude infected the cheering crowd, distracting them from the fact that none of them had a chance with the bachelor. Or maybe they'd already figured it out and were just happy to be here, partying while getting their chance to be on TV.

"I'm calling it," Thystle stated. "Matteo, you win."

He looked like he wanted to launch himself at me, but didn't dare take a step closer lest he lose control. Instead, he thrust the mic at Gaius, shot me a final intense stare that went straight to my dick, then disappeared behind the stage curtain.

I went straight to my hotel room after the second challenge ended. The urge to beat off was almost impossible to ignore, but I miraculously managed. I tempered the urge with the knowledge that it would be so much sweeter when Thystle was finally in my grasp.

The date was set for seven on the beach. As I showered and dressed, my blood vibrated in my veins. It was my first official date with Thystle—and unlike our secret tryst, this one would be filmed.

The anxiety from earlier snaked back around. The Dragonfate Games had exploded in popularity since season one. I'd blended into the background the first time around, but I'd lost all chance of that with Thystle. Our date would be broadcast, and I'd be front and center.

Vani and Keaux would see me. What would they think? Would they try to interfere? Or was I being paranoid for nothing?

My anxiety spiralled. Dammit, I'd done a decent job of holding it at bay until now.

I took a few deep breaths. I didn't have time for this shit. I had a date with a sexy alpha dragon.

Checking the time, I swore. Ten minutes until the date started. Where had the time gone? I didn't want to be late. I rushed out of the room—and instantly bumped into somebody.

Talon.

I frowned in confusion. "What are you doing here?"

"About time," Talon said under his breath. "You're going to be late."

I arched a brow. "I appreciate it, but that's not any of your business."

Talon stepped closer, scowling. He dropped all pretense

of friendliness. "Thystle doesn't deserve a man who's late," he muttered. "Or one who cheats."

"What the hell are you talking about?"

"You cheated during that challenge!" Talon snapped. "Nobody could've known those answers—except me." Oh, good gods. Was he wrapped up in his own delusion?

"I didn't cheat, thank you very much," I said mildly.

He shook his head. "You looked up the answers beforehand. I bet somebody on the inside fed you the questions."

Great. As if stealing my identity wasn't enough, now he'd cooked up conspiracy theories.

From the corner of my eye, I noticed the camera crew lurking behind corners. Conflict made excellent TV. But would they interfere if things got physical? I'd already gotten a pair of black eyes before security swooped in the first time.

"Nobody fed me anything. And I can't look up any of the answers. They took our cell phones when we landed," I reminded him.

Talon's eye twitched. He wasn't convinced. "You can hide things. Or just lie. Stop trying to fool Thystle. I'm the real Aquila."

Anger flared within me. I'd had enough of this.

"I'm not fooling him about anything," I shot back. "And if you *are* the real Aquila, you would've won the challenge."

"I was going to before Thystle asked me an impossible question!" Talon snapped.

At this point, my feathers were beyond ruffled, but I was done giving Talon any more of my time or energy. I knew the truth, and so did Thystle. I had no reason to convince Talon of anything.

"Then why are you threatened by me?" I asked calmly.

Talon narrowed his eyes. He wanted me to fight back, but I wouldn't give him that satisfaction.

"You know, I hate smug assholes like you," Talon spat.

Well, that came out of left field. I blinked, stunned by his sudden insult. How did someone even respond to that?

"I'm sorry you feel that way," I said.

He edged closer, his shoulders blocking the cameras from capturing the whole picture. I stood my ground. If he wanted to bully me, he'd have to step up his game. I'd already taken one beating during my time here. Hell, what was one more?

"There's nothing special about you," Talon muttered, glaring at me.

Despite the situation, I couldn't help but smile. "You're right. There isn't."

Talon seemed even more agitated that I'd agreed with him. His lip curled into a scowl. In a flurry of movement, he thrust the palm of his hand into my solar plexus. I coughed out a gasp as he shoved me against the wall. It didn't hurt, but it startled me.

"I don't know what Thystle sees in you," Talon growled. "He deserves better. He deserves—"

Thystle's knife-like voice cut through the air. "Tell me what I deserve."

My heart leapt into my throat, fluttering like a fledgling. Thystle stood at the end of the hallway. Fury radiated from him, filling the space and making him seem bigger than he was, like his dragon soul would burst free from his human skin any second.

Talon blanched. He leapt back from me, but it was obvious he was in my face seconds earlier. Plastering on a flashy grin, he said, "Good evening, Thystle."

"Answer the fucking question," Thystle snapped.

Talon visibly winced.

I bit my tongue to stop from chuckling. Poor guy. I would *not* want to be on an alpha dragon's bad side.

Standing up straighter, Talon said, "You deserve the best omega. A mate who is strong, capable, and talented."

Thystle didn't respond. He maintained his position, like a dark omen at the end of the hall. His glare was sharp enough to cut glass.

"And *you* are that omega, I presume?" he asked without intonation.

Talon thrust out his chin. "Of course. Like I tried to explain before, I'm the man of your dreams." He put a hand to his puffed-up chest. "I'm Aquila."

I had to admit, Talon was a good liar. He proclaimed it like a fact. Anybody else might've believed his story. Too bad he threw it in the face of two of the only people on this island who knew otherwise.

Thystle walked slowly towards us. Talon was frozen to the spot. Meanwhile, I lounged against the wall Talon pushed me against. I was pleased to watch this play out without getting involved. After all, Thystle had everything under control. Talon wouldn't dare utter another word or lay another hand on me while he was here.

Thystle shot me a playful glare. "You didn't show up, so I came to find out why." The warmth vanished from his gaze, turning icy as he focused it on Talon. "Tell me why you're harassing Matteo."

His order was ironclad. Not even Talon could talk his way out of it.

Talon sputtered. "I wasn't *harassing* him, we were having a friendly chat as fellow—"

"Oh, shut up," Thystle growled. "Don't play dumb. I saw you shove him."

The blood drained from Talon's face. "It wasn't—"

The vicious glare Thystle shot his way stopped him

mid-sentence. I stifled the urge to laugh. Talon looked like a kicked puppy.

As Thystle glanced at me, warmth and affection bloomed across his face. His sole focus was on me. It was like Talon didn't even exist.

"You were late to our date," Thystle accused, sounding more impatient than anything else.

I smiled. "Sorry."

He linked his arm in mine in a possessive gesture. Warm shivers shot up to my shoulder.

"Let's go," he ordered.

"Gladly," I replied.

I didn't look back over my shoulder as we left.

SIXTEEN

Thystle

AS WE LEFT THE HOTEL, I took a deep breath to clear the frustration in my lungs. I was still affected by the draconic edge, so when I blew it out, a puff of smoke filled the air.

"Wow. That was a big sigh," Matteo remarked.

"You have no clue how close I was to shifting back there," I grumbled. "If he'd touched you again, I would've lost my mind."

Matteo chuckled. "Good thing you didn't. I doubt your insurance would've covered total destruction of the hotel."

I snorted. "Dragon money fixes everything. Even complete hotel annihilation." I nuzzled his head. "How are you? Did he hurt you?"

Matteo smiled. "No, I'm fine. He just boasted at me. Don't worry."

I scowled. "Still. I didn't like that he put his hands on you." I butted my head against his again, craving physical contact. "Only I'm allowed to do that."

A soft laugh escaped him. "Is that right?"

"Yes," I replied grumpily. "And I'm pissed that so many other people have touched you except me."

Matteo grinned. "Then clearly you should touch me more."

"I will," I promised.

Matteo's eyes flashed with desire. The feeling was mutual. More than anything I wanted to tackle him to the ground, rip his clothes off, and have my way with him.

Too bad we had a public, filmed date to attend to.

I suddenly felt the gentle touch of Matteo's hand on my arm. "Thank you, Thystle. For saving me."

My protective instinct flared up. I pulled Matteo closer. "I won't let anybody hurt you. You're mine. Besides, I waited for you for ten whole minutes."

He looked amused. "Ten minutes? That's what you consider being late?"

"It's a long time when I miss you every waking second."

Matteo blinked, his brown eyes warm. "Thystle... That's sweet."

"It's true." Catching a note of shampoo, I leaned over and sniffed him. "Did you shower since I last saw you?"

"Was I not supposed to?" he asked.

"You can, if you want. I just love your natural scent."

A flush bloomed across his cheeks. "I'll remember that next time."

When we reached the set of the date, Matteo whistled. "Wow. They did this in a couple hours?"

The game show set had disappeared, replaced by a rustic stage decorated with fairy lights and bright pops of color in the form of flowers.

"I remember this," Matteo commented. "Taylor won a date with Crimson on season one. I always thought the moonlit date was particularly romantic."

A growl rumbled in my throat as I held him tighter. "Fuck Crimson. Our date will be way better."

He laughed airily. "Of course it will, because it's with you."

We stepped onto the platform arm-in-arm. A single table with two chairs stood in the center draped in a crisp white cloth. The sea breeze rustled the fairy lights, filling the air with the delicate scent of salt.

I walked over to one of the chairs, pulling it out for Matteo. He flashed me a smile as he took a seat.

I took the opposite one, content to stare at him while our server appeared.

"Uh oh, here comes trouble," Gaius greeted us teasingly.

I raised a brow at him. He wore a white waiter's apron on top of his gaudy bright yellow shirt.

"What are you doing here?" I asked.

He fake sighed. "My dragon overlords have me doing double-duty." Grinning, he produced menus. "There you go, boys."

I wondered if somebody put Gaius up to this stint, or if he was doing it for fun. It was hard to tell with him. He was like a positive wildcard, compared to my brother, Viol, who was a terrifying one.

"I'll leave you alone for a minute," Gaius said. He winked, then sauntered off.

I blew out a breath. "Finally. Nobody around to bother us."

Matteo chuckled. "Until Gaius comes back for our orders."

"Screw him," I said, waving a hand. At the same time, I edged my foot closer to his beneath the table and gave it a playful nudge.

Matteo arched a brow, picking up the menu. "Come on, that's not nice."

"I'm sick of being nice," I mumbled. "I want to be alone with you."

He didn't respond, but shot me a lopsided grin as he pushed his foot against mine. It was a small gesture, but it went straight to my dick. I was *this* close to flipping the table and cancelling the moonlit beach date in exchange for a raunchy night of fucking.

But then I saw the way Matteo looked at me, and my heart skipped a beat. It was full of softness, of want. He lived blissfully in the moment. That tamped down my impatience to speed through the date.

The camera crew lurked around the edge of the stage. I noticed Matteo glanced at them once in a while, as if uneasy about something. But he was filmed the entire time he was here, and he'd been on a whole other season of TV. Hell, he was a former music god. Wasn't he used to the attention?

"Something bugging you?" I asked.

His eyes flicked back to me instantly. "No," he said with the slightest hint in his voice that he wasn't telling the full truth. But before I could dig deeper, he reached across the table and put his hand on top of mine. The resulting shivers shooting up my arm distracted me. "It's nice to be with you like this. No crowd, no competition. It's almost like we're having a normal date."

I tilted my head. "Is that what you prefer? Normalcy?"

He shrugged. "It's just what I'm used to."

I put my other palm on top of Matteo's, sandwiching him between my hands. "Well, nothing about you is *normal* to me. You're amazing in every possible way."

A blush danced across his cheeks. The swelling around his eyes had all but disappeared, putting his beautiful brown eyes on full display. There was no doubt about who he was anymore. Those were the same eyes that watched over me every night from that glossy poster. The man before me was a decade older, but he was still the Aquila I fell in love with, the one I obsessed over.

I squeezed his hand tighter. Now that he was in my grasp, I would never, *ever* let him go.

"Made up your minds, boys?" Gaius asked, popping up beside us like a whack-a-mole.

I hadn't even looked at the menu. How could I when Matteo was right across from me? It would be like ordering food from a delivery app while standing in front of the Mona Lisa.

"I don't care," I said. "Double the portion of whatever Matteo's getting. We'll share."

Matteo smiled, apparently amused by my one-track mind. "All right," he said, using his non-grasped hand to give the menu back to Gaius. "We'll share the sushi platter."

"An excellent choice!" Gaius said, gathering the menus. "Though, I doubt even the exquisite food will steal Thystle's attention away from you."

"What'd you say?" I asked.

He pranced off. "Nothing. I'm gone now!"

I leaned forward, wanting to be closer to Matteo. I could've stared at him the entire time, but I knew it was my responsibility as the alpha bachelor to lead the conversation. Stupid TV etiquette.

"So, how have the Games been for you so far?" I asked.

Matteo tilted his head thoughtfully. "Very different from season one."

"In a bad way?"

"Not at all. Eventful would be a better word," he corrected. "It's more excitement than I'm used to."

That was an odd thing to say. Matteo was literally a superstar. He toured, sang at sold out concerts, and was swarmed by fans at every single meet-and-greet. He was fucking *Aquila*, for Holy Drake's sake. How could a crappy game show be exciting to him?

Then again, he'd been out of the spotlight for ten years, and I still didn't know why. I itched to ask him. I wanted to know both as a fan and as somebody who cared for him. The circumstances of TalonStorm's break up were cloudy, and no clear answer *why* ever surfaced in the media and tabloids. No matter what happened, a big life change like that couldn't have been easy.

"But don't get me wrong," Matteo said, stroking the top of my hand with his thumb. "I'm having the time of my life here with you, Thystle."

My heart stuttered. Fuck, I could've grabbed his face and kissed him, but that wasn't allowed. Not on camera, anyway. I imagined a miniature version of Jade in my mind, shaking his head and wagging his finger disapprovingly at me. That was enough to narrowly dodge the impulse... for now.

It was fine. Once darkness fell and this date was over, I fully intended on breaking the rules.

"I feel the same way," I said. "If that wasn't glaringly obvious."

He chuckled, a soft blush dusting his cheeks. "I figured." He paused, gaze going distant as he appeared to gather his thoughts. "You know, there's something—"

His beautiful voice was interrupted by a loud, jarring yell. The nails-on-chalkboard sound irked me. When I turned around, I saw the last thing I wanted to see—Talon, running straight for us with a triumphant expression. Security kobolds ran after him, but Talon's long legs afforded him a greater stride. They couldn't keep up.

My dragon soul swelled inside me. It crackled beneath the surface of my skin, keen to break free and put an end to this bullshit. But Talon was great at making an ass out of himself. I may as well let him say his piece. It was good TV.

Besides, Matteo was safe behind me. I'd never let that man touch him, or even speak to him again. All Matteo needed to do was say the word and I'd bite his head off—figuratively, of course.

Unless he wanted me to do it literally. I'd do that, too.

I looked over my shoulder. Matteo rested his chin on his hands and sighed. He looked equally sick of Talon's BS.

"I'm gonna deal with the situation. I'll be back in a minute," I promised Matteo.

He nodded. "Don't take too long. This is still *our* date, remember?"

My heart beat toppled over itself at the sultry look Matteo shot me. That man was going to get it in bed later.

"Oh, I know," I said with a grin. "I wouldn't give up a date with you for anything."

Talon stomped up to the edge of the stage. I leapt over the edge of the platform and landed on the sand to face him. I crossed my arms, hoping to convey how pissed I was.

Before he could launch into his rant, I warned, "You know, this is the second time you've interrupted this particular date. Whatever you have to say better be worth it."

Talon's face twisted into a smug grin. "Oh, it will. Trust me, Thystle. You're going to want to hear this."

I didn't like his tone, or the way he smirked in Matteo's direction.

"Spit it out," I ordered. Every second wasted on him was a second I could've spent with Matteo.

With a crazed expression, Talon suddenly reached into his pocket and yanked out a cell phone—something he wasn't allowed to have. The screen was lit up with text and pictures. Talon thrust it towards me like some kind of checkmate.

I narrowed my eyes without really looking at it. For now, I ignored the fact that he had a forbidden phone, since I wanted to get to the point faster.

"What exactly am I looking at?" I asked.

"An article about the real reason TalonStorm broke up," Talon sneered. "I found it online."

I resisted the urge to curl my lip into a snarl. "And?"

Talon let the question linger in the air, letting it fester and draw attention to him. If he spent any longer belea-guering this point, I was going to snap.

Then, Talon raised his cell phone screen. It was opened to a skeezy tabloid article released just this morn-ing. The sensational headline grabbed my eyes: FORMER TALONSTORM STAR APPEARS ON REALITY DATING SHOW...AGAIN!

Beneath the sensational headline, there were two photos side by side, clearly of the same person. One was in full performance costuming—the other was a normal man in everyday clothes.

My fated mate. Matteo.

A jolt went through me. Matteo largely went unnoticed in season one. He did too good of a job disappearing into the background. Season two hadn't aired yet, but Talon had a cell phone. He was spiteful towards Matteo's ease during the quiz show, so he played detective to try and drag him down.

The phone also explained Talon's own suspiciously good performance during the quiz. He must've looked up widely-known information about me beforehand. Dirty cheater.

Regardless, I was mostly pissed Talon had outed

Matteo against his will. It made me hate this bastard even more.

"The reason TalonStorm broke up," Talon said conspiratorially, "is all because of Aquila. Or should I say, Matteo?"

SEVENTEEN

Matteo

MY BLOOD RAN cold as Talon uttered those words. My stomach flipped and my palms turned clammy. Guilt I'd tamped down into dirt came rushing back. I felt like the last ten years of emotional progress hadn't happened—I was thrust into the past, just as upset and broken-hearted as I was back then.

How would Thystle feel when he found out the truth?

My insecurities warred with my need to remain close to Thystle. I wanted to run. I wanted to stay.

My gut instinct said *stay*.

You know he's your alpha.

He will protect you.

I took a deep breath. Every muscle in my body wanted to run, to shift and fly away, but my heart opposed it. My soul believed in Thystle.

Despite the anxiety swamping my stomach, I forced myself to confront reality.

Thystle stood across from Talon. I could see Talon's face, but not Thystle's since his back was to me. The other omega continued to wear that smug grin. He thought he'd won.

Maybe he had. I wouldn't know until Thystle said something.

Thystle raised his arm, silently asking for Talon's phone. Talon handed it over as proof of my crime. He reminded me of a snitching child, eager to be praised.

Thystle glanced down to read the screen. The longer he stayed silent, the more stressed I became.

As awful as Talon's disruption felt, his declaration wasn't technically false. Would Thystle ever forgive me for being the reason TalonStorm disbanded? All I could do was wait and see.

"Gaius," Thystle finally said without lifting his head.

The gryphon shifter popped up behind me. He leapt over the stage, standing next to Thystle. "Yes?"

Thystle handed him the phone. "Add this to the safe of confiscated items. He can have it back when he's packed to leave on the flight home—which I want arranged for later tonight."

Talon's jaw dropped. "What?" he sputtered.

"Maybe I wasn't clear," Thystle said, his voice dripping venom. "You're out. Not only did you break the rules, you harassed and physically assaulted another contestant."

Pure disbelief spread over Talon's face. "You're not serious. I barely touched him!"

"So, you *did* touch him," Thystle growled. "Go back to the hotel and pack your shit. I've wasted enough time entertaining you."

My heart experienced whiplash. The terror I'd felt seconds ago melted away into desperate relief. I sank into the chair as the tension evaporated from my body.

Talon didn't move. He looked torn between anger and shock. "That's it? You don't care *he* was the reason your favorite band broke up?"

A draconic edge slithered into Thystle's voice. "What

part of *go back to the hotel* don't you understand? Don't push me, Talon. If you say one more thing about Matteo, you might regret it."

"Erm, Thystle," Gaius said under his breath. "You shouldn't really threaten the contestants..."

"It's not a threat," Thystle growled. "It's a promise."

Gaius sighed in defeat. Clearly, there was no arguing with an enraged dragon.

"Fine. I'll leave. Give me back my phone," Talon snapped. He snatched it from Gaius, who didn't bother keeping it away from him. "Just know this. You're making a huge mistake, Thystle. Matteo is nothing but trouble!"

My heart turned to lead, sinking into the pit of my stomach. I didn't know what was said in the article, but I doubted it was far from the truth. Vani and Keaux, my former friends and band members, telling their version of what happened the day TalonStorm broke up.

Because of me.

Thystle was dead silent. The security and camera crew stayed frozen to the spot, waiting for his reaction. I didn't dare breathe.

All of a sudden, Thystle shoved Gaius backwards. I barely had a second to wonder why—in a flash of twisting bones and magic, Thystle's form changed. His dragon self exploded out of his human flesh. The handsome man disappeared, swallowed up by a massive, lithe dragon with glittering amethyst scales. Spikes of darker purple rose up along his spine, and black talons jutted out from his scaly paws.

When the shift completed, Thystle reared his head and punched out a terrifying roar that I felt in my bones.

Talon swore and stumbled back, falling on his ass in the sand. Meanwhile, the camera crew crowded closer, getting the best shots of Thystle's dragon transformation.

During the chaos, Gaius ended up beside me, chuckling. "There he goes. That's how you know a dragon *really* likes you."

A fluttery sensation wrapped around my ribs. Did Thystle want to protect me so badly he couldn't control his transformation? That was the sweetest thing anyone had ever done for me.

"Stand up," Thystle ordered Talon, his voice distorted in his dragon form.

Talon staggered to his feet, clearing his throat and dusting the sand off his rump as he tried to recoup his dignity. "Well, what do you think about what I've told you?"

Smoke trailed from Thystle's nostrils as he snorted. "I think you can shove it up your ass."

Talon made a face. Sensing he hit a brick wall with Thystle, he glared at me instead. "You know what you did!"

How was I supposed to respond? I doubted Talon actually cared about the band drama. He only cared about it as leverage. He wanted to hurt me because Thystle liked me, not him.

A deep growl reverberated in Thystle's chest. He sidestepped in front of me, blocking me from Talon's line of sight.

"I'm *this* close to getting security involved," Thystle warned. "Now, get."

I couldn't see Talon, but I assumed he trudged off with a pout. Once he was further away, I noticed the security kobolds escorting him back to the hotel.

"Don't worry," Gaius told me. "They'll make sure he doesn't make any more trouble. I've already messaged Duke and Jade about getting him a flight home later tonight."

I let out a sigh of relief. "Thanks."

Thystle turned around. It wasn't my first time seeing his dragon form, but it was my first time seeing it up close and personal. A shiver ran down my spine. He was exquisite. There was no other way to describe him. His long, narrow snout was coated in a thousand tiny scales, all shimmering like gemstones beneath the fairy lights. His eyes shared that mesmerizing color. They burned as he stared at me.

Desire radiated from him like heat from a fire. Dragon form or not, I could tell he wanted to throw me down against the stage and fuck me.

Unfortunately, the cameras still lingered, so he settled for the next best thing. He nuzzled his head into my chest, making a sound oddly close to a purr.

"I'm sorry you had to deal with that," he grumbled. The dragon form altered his voice, making it thick and gravelly.

I stroked his scales. The cool sensation calmed me. "I should say the same about you."

His lip curled, revealing sharp rows of fangs. "It was my pleasure to get rid of that dickhead. I only wished I'd done it earlier."

My stomach twisted.

"I want to talk about what he said," I murmured.

Thystle's eyes flashed. "Do you want to do it privately?"

I smiled, warmed by his offer. "No, it's okay. If there's tabloids about it, then it's time to share my side of the story."

He flicked his tail thoughtfully, as if debating whether to shoo away the camera crew or not. Ultimately, he respected my decision to let them stay.

"Let's at least talk somewhere roomier so I don't crush the stage," Thystle suggested.

I grinned. "What, you can't change back?"

"No," Thystle said bluntly. "I'm too riled up."

I bumped my forehead against his. "That's fine. I like you in this form, anyways."

He made that draconic purring sound again. He offered a dexterous paw, careful of his gigantic claws, leading me off the stage. Once we found a spot to sit in the sand, Thystle curled his huge body protectively around me. I rested my full weight against him with a content sigh. It was nice laying against a dragon. Despite the coolness of his scales, his side was strangely warm. I could've cuddled him forever.

A bonus of Thystle's big, pillowy body was that I couldn't see the cameras anymore. Honestly, I forgot they existed. That made it easier to spill my heart out to Thystle.

I took a deep breath and gathered my thoughts. I'd run away from this for so long, but now it finally caught up to me.

As if reading my mind, Thystle nuzzled my cheek. "I'm here," he promised.

No use tiptoeing around it anymore. I had to take a leap of faith right off the deep end.

"It started ten years ago, when all three of us were in our early twenties," I began. "TalonStorm was in its stride."

"I remember," Thystle said wistfully.

"We were all high off stardom. We felt untouchable, like we ruled the world. But with that stardom came arrogance. It affected all of us."

"I can't imagine *you* being arrogant," Thystle remarked.

I let out a dry chuckle. "I'm glad you didn't know me back then. I was... a mess. Behind the scenes, we drank and partied too hard. You know, typical dumb stuff you do as a young celebrity."

Thystle tilted his head. "I never thought about that. I always assumed you guys had the coolest lives."

"That depends on your definition of cool," I mused. "It was fun for a while, sure, but I got sick of it."

"You got sick of making music?" Thystle asked. He sounded heartbroken.

I shook my head. "No. Never. My art was my passion. But I got sick of the drama, the paparazzi, the gossip, the marketing, the endless pushing from agents..." A haggard sigh escaped me as I leaned further into Thystle's side. "It got to me."

Thystle let out a sympathetic growl as he nuzzled my cheek. "I'm sorry, Matteo. I had no idea the lifestyle was so hard on you."

I gave him a half-smile. "It wouldn't have been so bad if I had a support system. But the people who were supposed to be there for me... weren't. Vani and Keaux felt differently about the lifestyle. They loved it."

"So, what happened?" Thystle asked.

"One night, I decided to tell them the truth. I never wanted to quit TalonStorm, or stop making music. I just wanted to slow down, to put the brakes on the hard-and-fast shit. I didn't want us to crash and burn." My gaze fell to the sand as the memories came back to me. I found myself stroking Thystle's scales like I was petting a therapy dog. "And... there was something else. I wanted to find my fated mate."

His amethyst gaze flashed. "You say that like it was a problem."

"It was," I explained. "They didn't want to hear

anything about finding a partner, or settling down. They thought it'd take away from our non-stop party lifestyle."

A puzzled growl rumbled in Thystle's throat. "But why? Doesn't every shifter want to find their fated mate? It's instinct."

There it was. The big lie.

I turned to face him. "Vani and Keaux aren't shifters. They're humans. Out of the three members of Talon-Storm, I was the only shifter. The odd one out."

Thystle stared at me wide-eyed, like I'd tilted his entire world on its axis. He groaned and put a paw to his forehead.

"But TalonStorm was supposed to be a shifter band," he said. "What about the animal masks, the costumes?"

"That's all they were. Masks. An act. Vani and Keaux just pretended to be shifters. It was part of the marketing. After all, who'd ever know, right? It's not like society encourages us to shift into our animal forms. Not even celebrities." I sighed, rubbing my arm. "I can't really blame them for lying, though. It was our agent who suggested it as a way to stand out from other bands at the time. It's hard to say no when someone in the business tells you to do something."

Thystle's forked tongue stuck out as he hissed. "I can't believe this. No wonder they didn't understand your instincts."

I nodded sadly. "The night I told them, they both lost it. They accused me of being arrogant, because I was the lead singer and face of the band." I stared up at the star-speckled sky. "Maybe it was my fault for telling them that night. We'd all had too much to drink, and I was really in my feelings."

"It is *not* your fault that they freaked out," Thystle

assured me. "They were your friends. They should've made the effort to understand you."

A lump formed in my throat. This whole conversation felt like ripping open an unhealed wound, yet Thystle's support made it easier. I wouldn't have been able to discuss this with anyone else. That was why I kept it to myself for so long.

But baring my heart to a dragon? Totally doable.

"What happened next?" Thystle urged.

"We all blew up. There was an explosive argument that night." I grimaced at the memory. "I figured we could sleep it off and regroup to talk the next morning, but that didn't happen. Instead, Vani and Keaux kicked me out of TalonStorm. They didn't want me in the band anymore, so they dissolved it instead."

All of Thystle's spines flared. "Are you serious? That's total bullshit!"

"I thought so, too. But they were too angry to listen. They'd made up their minds."

"Did you fight back?" Thystle demanded.

"How could I? It was two humans against one shifter." I drew up my knees to my chest. "It was a big, ugly misunderstanding I wished never happened."

A sympathetic growl reverberated in Thystle's throat as he rubbed his snout against my cheek. "I'm so sorry. I had no idea. When TalonStorm broke up, I was too devastated to find out why. I hate knowing it caused you so much pain."

A sigh escaped me, but it felt good, like letting go of the past. "It's all right. It's taken a while, but I'm slowly getting over it." I smiled at him. "Talking it out with you helps."

He curled his tail closer. "That's what I'm here for."

My heart skipped. Thystle hadn't said anything particularly romantic, but those feelings pooled around me in waves. He cared about me deeply, on a level I'd never experienced from anyone else—and I felt the same way about him.

He didn't *need* to spell it out for me to understand. It was the little things he did that drew me to him, that made me wonder if my quest for a fated mate finally reached its conclusion...

Holding Thystle's dragon head in my hands, I pressed my nose against his. His breath had a smoky aroma, like a campfire.

"If it's all right," I whispered, quiet enough for the mics to miss. "I'd like to be alone with you."

Thystle's pupils squeezed into narrow slits, and I felt the barely perceptible tension seizing his body.

The dragon's response was a low growl, barely voiced and feral. "Go to your hotel room. In an hour, you're *mine*."

EIGHTEEN

Thystle

FIFTY-NINE MINUTES LATER, I was on his balcony.

Containing my dragon was a colossal effort, like shoving a crocodile into a cat crate. I'd flown to Matteo's room, shifted as I landed, then gave the sliding door a single knock. I *needed* to change back. My human body couldn't handle the emotion and desire raging within me. It clawed at my insides, desperate to be freed.

Matteo didn't make me wait. He opened the door and silently met my gaze. A glassy desire clouded his dark eyes.

Without a word, I grabbed his wrist, pulled him to my chest, and leapt off the balcony. Having Matteo in my grasp was the straw that broke the camel's back. My dragon soul burst free, ripping through the strained seams of my human form. I stretched my wings to their limit. I loved the way the night air felt beneath my leathery flesh.

I wasn't alone in shifting. The sky worked its magic on Matteo, too. As we took to the air together, he slipped into his golden eagle form. The tips of our wings touched as we flew side-by-side. His eagle form was gorgeous. His beautiful brown eyes caught the moonlight, making them gleam, and his feathers had a pale sheen that made him look like he glowed.

"I want to lock talons and sky-dive with you," I said suddenly.

Matteo let out a few clicks of laughter. "That's bald eagles, not golden eagles. But I won't say no to a good courtship ritual."

My heart soared—then, so did I. Pumping my muscles, I flew upwards. Matteo joined me in our ascent. The air cooled the higher we went. The hotel and beach shrank beneath us. I felt exhilarated—up this high, it felt like me and Matteo were in our own private world. I forgot the Games, the challenges, the drama. Right now, it was me and him.

My mate.

Facing him, I extended my front claws. Matteo banked his wings, coming closer, then locked his talons in mine.

"Ready?" he asked.

"Ready."

Together, we tipped into a free fall. Our bodies spun in a rhythmic spiral, a twister of feathers and scales. Wind rushed around us. It was a wild, intoxicating feeling. I gripped Matteo's talons harder and pulled him as close as possible. We were one unit, a knife slicing the air. He cried out in a screech of laughter, and I joined him with a roar.

We plummeted towards the beach. It only took a few seconds, but the experience felt longer. Right before we'd crash, we disconnected our talons, flared our wings, and took proper flight.

But I wasn't done with Matteo yet. I beckoned him with a deep growl, wanting him to follow me. He let out a few affirmative piping notes as he flew by my side.

That breathtaking courtship ritual lit a fire in my blood. I was full to the brim with desire, and this time, no amount of willpower could dampen it. Hell, I couldn't even wait until we reached my bedroom.

I was going to claim Matteo once and for all, and it had to be *now*.

We soared over the forest until I spotted a glint of pale light. A secluded pond in a clearing reflected the moonlight. I nudged Matteo with the tip of my wing and flew down. He followed behind me, shifting to human form as he touched down on the dewy grass. He gazed around the misty clearing, taking in the sights and smells of the untouched forest oasis.

"This is gorgeous," he murmured.

Unlike him, I hadn't shifted. I remained in my dragon form as I pressed my maw against his cheek.

"Not as gorgeous as you," I growled.

He stroked the sides of my long, scaly face. "Are you flirting with me?"

I huffed, tendrils of smoke wafting from my nostrils. "When *aren't* I flirting with you?"

Matteo pressed his forehead to my face. The scent of his breath and the warmth of his body made my blood sizzle. A sultry growl reverberated in my throat. Unable to stop myself, I stepped forward while Matteo clung to my face. The motion swung his body backward, and I lowered him gently to the ground. He gazed up at me, his brown eyes warm and shimmering.

My dragon soul flared like a night sky full of fireworks. My claws dug into the ground around Matteo's body, and I nuzzled my face against his, soaking up the scent and heat of his body.

"You're mine," I growled against his neck.

He shivered. "Is that so?"

"You're teasing me, but I mean it."

"I am teasing," Matteo said, eyes flashing with amusement, "because I want you to *show* me." That was all he had to say.

I parted my maw, letting my long wet tongue slip out to lap against Matteo's lips. A soft sound escaped him as he opened his mouth to accommodate me. Despite my ravenous hunger, I took it slow, easing my tongue within. Matteo's quiet whimpers turned into a moan. He kissed back, wrapping his human tongue around my dragon one.

A thousand erupting volcanoes weren't as hot as my blood. Arousal shot down the base of my sinuous spine, culminating in an excited flick of my tail. I unfurled my wings, containing Matteo within their span. My claws inched deeper into the dirt as I struggled to keep my desire in check.

Matteo suddenly grabbed my face and thrust his tongue as deep as it would go. I growled in pleasant surprise. His human tongue was small compared to mine, but it felt incredible. The wet heat of his mouth and the delicious taste of him sent shock waves of arousal through my system.

The kiss ended when Matteo pulled off, gasping for breath. My dragon lungs were a lot bigger than his.

"I win," I teased.

He huffed. "Yeah?"

Then he grabbed my face, kissing me passionately again. His tongue battled against mine with hotter fervor, but in the end, I won a second time. Matteo gasped, panting hard as he collapsed on the grass.

And his panting wasn't the only thing that was hard. As I glanced down, I noticed his raging hard on.

Satisfaction filled me. I grinned widely. "Two make-out sessions are all it takes, huh?"

Still fighting for breath, Matteo arched a brow. "I wouldn't be so smug, dragon. Take a look at yourself."

I blinked in confusion. Dragons didn't have visible erections the way humans did—not unless my hemipenes slipped out of my cloaca without me noticing.

I turned my head upside-down, glanced down at my lower half... then promptly realized Matteo was right.

I gawked at the two slinky dragon cocks that jutted out of the slit in my scales. When the hell did that happen?

Matteo smirked. "I win."

I hissed playfully, then licked his face. "This round."

He angled his neck to stare at my hemipenes curiously. "So, are those going in next?"

I snorted. "No."

He sounded a bit disappointed. "Why not?"

"Because unless you want to turn into a Matteo-kebab, it's physically impossible," I explained.

"Not even one?"

I arched a scaly brow. "Can you fit an eight-foot long toy inside you?" He paused for a second. "Point taken."

I licked his lips. "If you *really* want to try it some time, we can, but you've gotta work yourself up first, size queen."

"Fair enough," he conceded. "But I'm not done with them yet..."

To my surprise, Matteo slid beneath my belly scales. Anticipation prickled my skin as Matteo wriggled underneath me.

He wasn't going *there*, was he?

Just as I mulled over that thought, I sucked in a sharp breath.

Yeah, he definitely went there.

Matteo had wrapped his lips around the tip of one of my cocks. The shock of pleasure that coursed through my system made me growl. A shudder scurried down my spine, making me dig my claws deeper into the ground.

His wet mouth was gentle yet firm as he sucked and licked my sensitive flesh.

A growl-purr escaped me. The deep sound reverberated through the clearing, sending ripples of vibration over the pond's surface.

My draconic side took over. Even if I wanted to, I couldn't speak. The pleasure melted my brain and turned me feral. I could barely *think*, much less voice anything resembling a sentence.

Matteo moved off my cock with a soft *pop*. "How do you like that?"

I growled.

"Is that... good?" he asked.

I growled deeper, hoping to get the point across.

He chuckled. "Oh, no. I broke Thystle."

I arched my neck around the side of my body to glare at him. I met his gaze, then gave him an encouraging shove with my snout.

Holy Drake, Matteo looked so fucking hot. His lips were wet and swollen, and his cheeks were flushed. As much as I enjoyed the dragon blowjob, I didn't know how long I'd last. The dam holding back my control was about to burst. I wouldn't be satisfied until I stuffed him full of my cock.

But I wasn't about to let this beautiful sight go to waste. Matteo got the hint. Still meeting my eyes, he inched forward to wrap his lips around one of my cocks. I let out a soft bellow of pleasure. The cock Matteo sucked on was longer than the height of his entire body, but that didn't stop him from worshiping the tip of it. He swallowed as much as he physically could without choking, bobbing his head back and forth. Saliva dripped from the corners of his mouth. His cheeks hollowed as he sucked me off fervently.

Just when I felt *too* close, Matteo broke off with a gasp for air. But he wasn't done. He smirked, eyes flashing. A different air came over him, almost like he'd shifted, yet he remained in human form.

"Did you ever fantasize about this, Thystle?" Matteo asked, his voice rough. "About Aquila sucking your cock?"

My pulse surged. I felt delirious, pushed to the edge of sanity. I wanted to close my jaws lovingly around Matteo and never let him go.

"Yes," I growled through my teeth.

His smug grin widened. "You wanted me on my knees in front of you. You fantasized about how good it would feel."

My moan came out as a soft roar. Hot pleasure pooled in the pit of my stomach.

That damned tease.

I bucked my hips, shoving one of my cocks against his face in a not-so-subtle demand for more. Matteo let out a breathy laugh.

"Greedy dragon," he said. "You want me to suck you off that badly?"

"*Yes*," I hissed.

Matteo's wet mouth enveloped me. I threw my head back and roared loud enough for it to echo. Spikes of pleasure rocketed through my skull. My breath came out in choppy growls and huffs. I lost my fucking mind.

Matteo pushed me to the brink of exploding, but I wasn't done with him yet. In a flash, I shifted back to human form. He blinked, startled at the sudden change, but when I pinned him to the ground, his eyes flashed in understanding. I grabbed his thighs and hiked them up over my shoulders. I was glad his clothes disappeared during his earlier shift and no staff had been present to replace them. Now I had full, instant access to his ass.

After I shifted to human form, my two dragon cocks became one raging erection, but it didn't dull my animal-istic desire to fuck Matteo senseless. My fingers dug into his thighs as I lined up the head of my dick with Matteo's drenched, twitching hole. He was ready for me.

"I'm going to fuck you," I ground out between haggard breaths.

Matteo looked as eager to receive as I was to give. He grabbed my thighs to brace himself for the incoming thrusts.

"Don't just fuck me," Matteo muttered. "Breed me."

That went straight to my cock. I groaned as it twitched, desperate to be inside of him already.

But the words gave me pause. It was a drop of clarity that put a stop to my frenzy.

"Breed you," I repeated. "Is that dirty talk, or...?"

Matteo levelled a steady look at me. "Thystle. That's the whole point of the Dragonfate Games, isn't it? So you can find a proper mate?"

I blinked slowly. Among all the chaos of the TV production, silly challenges, and contestant drama, that important fact slipped my mind. Matteo was right. This whole charade was meant to unite a pair of fated mates and start a family.

Matteo sat up and grasped my hands, staring into my eyes. "That's what I've wanted from the very beginning. I want it all with you." He leaned close enough that I could see the moonlight reflected in his warm brown eyes. "As your fated mate, I want to carry your egg."

My heart fluttered like a thousand dragon wingbeats.

"Matteo. I've known you were mine since the second I laid eyes on you, back when I only knew you as Aquila. Nobody understood my obsession, but I *knew*. And now you're here in my grasp. I can finally hold you, and touch you, and love you the way you deserve. There's no hiding from your fated alpha dragon mate," I teased.

A smile lit up his face. "Thystle..."

I gave him a chaste, yet romantic kiss on the lips. "Sooner or later, I'd always find you. Now there's no escape."

"Who said I wanted to escape?" Grinning, Matteo spread his legs. "It's quite the opposite. Like I said, I want you to breed me."

My arousal flared to life. "Then get ready."

The mating urge consumed me. As I pressed the head of my cock against Matteo's entrance, it easily slipped inside.

Matteo downed a sharp gulp of air, then hissed through his teeth as his body adjusted to my intrusion.

"Are you all right?" I asked.

Matteo grinned. "It's no eight-foot long toy, but you're still pretty damn big."

Worried I hurt him, I went to pull out, but Matteo grabbed my wrists.

"If you pull out, I'll quit the Games," he warned with a sharp glare.

I snorted. "Fine, you diva."

Matteo moved his hips, then sighed when he found the perfect angle. I felt his muscles relax when he was fully comfortable.

"Now, fuck me," he ordered.

The demand sparked in my brain like a lightning strike. Fueled by possessiveness and desire, I grabbed Matteo's hips. I was about to make him mine in every way.

My cock sank deeper into Matteo's wet, needy hole. He let out a half-gasp, half-moan. His tight hole pulsated around my sensitive shaft, sending passive shocks of pleasure up my spine.

My dragon rumbled in my soul, simultaneously pleased and greedy for more. It wouldn't pipe down until I'd flooded Matteo's insides with my cum.

Which was exactly what I intended to do.

Matteo's little gasps and moans nearly made me salivate. The way his chest arched, and the way his damp hair fell across his forehead was so sexy. Did he have any fucking clue how hot he was?

All my years of pent-up crushing and lusting over Aquila exploded. My hips thrusted wildly. I felt savage, deranged. I was completely out of control over my fated mate.

"Fuck, Thystle," Matteo choked out.

The raw desire in his voice was gas thrown on the fire of my lust. As I plowed him harder, his moans grew louder and drawn-out to the point where he practically screamed.

"Fuck," Matteo breathed, barely voicing the word. His expression was dazed. Sweat rolled down his temples and his cheeks were flushed.

Holy Drake, I wanted a photo of him right at this moment. For reasons.

"Shit," Matteo gasped out. A roguish glint flashed across his eyes. "Getting fucked by my number-one fan feels so good..."

I blushed, then grinned. "You fucking tease."

Matteo dug his heels into my lower back, locking me into place. "I'm not teasing." His voice was husky with arousal. "Breed me, fanboy. Pump your beloved Aquila full of cum and knock him up."

Drake-fucking-dammit.

He knew exactly what turned me on, didn't he?

That naughty talk was enough to send me careening over the edge. My nails dug into Matteo's skin as I lurched forward, thrusting my cock into the deepest part of him. A feral, draconic cry tore from my throat as I finished inside my mate. Just beneath it, I heard Matteo's mirror cry and felt a splash of warm wetness against my belly.

After the stars disappeared from my vision, I curled up beside him. His hair was mussed up in that attractive, I-just-had-sex way. With his rockstar hair and loving smile, he looked halfway between Matteo and Aquila. He was both.

And they were both mine.

NINETEEN

Matteo

AFTER A THOROUGH SHOWER TO rinse off last night's evidence, I headed down to the lobby to meet the rest of the contestants. It surprised me to notice how much the number of people shrank. So much had changed since before the Games began. I'd come into this experience with a glimmer of hope, a fantasy of finding my fated mate... and now I had him.

A smile crept onto my face as I thought of Thystle. Last night was magical, and it was only the beginning of our lifelong love.

I yawned loudly. The sex was amazing, but it *did* keep me up past my usual bedtime.

"That's the third time you've yawned," Alaric pointed out. "Stayed up late?"

I stood up straighter. I hadn't noticed the slinky cat shifter's approach.

"Couldn't sleep," I said, which was true enough. It would be impossible to fall asleep while Thystle bred me.

Alaric eyed me shrewdly. He lowered his voice to a low mumble. "As a bird shifter, you probably can't tell, but you have the distinct smell of dragon on you."

Shame flushed my cheeks. Dammit. I thought I did a decent job of getting rid of it.

I didn't want to lie to Alaric, especially when he already knew. Besides, I was sick of hiding the truth.

"I'm sorry," I said honestly.

I didn't apologize for what I'd done, but because I felt sorry for Alaric. He was clearly lonely and yearning.

He shrugged. "Why? You found your fated mate. That's why we're here."

There was no disappointment in his tone, only acceptance with a hint of jealousy. I didn't blame him. It couldn't be easy competing in the Dragonfate Games twice to no avail.

"You'll find your mate, Alaric," I said. "Don't give up."

He arched a well-groomed brow. "Who said I was giving up? I *will* get my dragon mate, mark my words."

I smiled, happy to hear his determination.

"I heard Talon made an ass out of himself last night," Alaric commented. A smirk played on his lips.

I barely withheld a snort. "That's one way to put it."

A familiar lithe figure wriggled through the crowd towards us. Muzo appeared with a big grin, dragging a grimacing Poppy behind him.

"Hey! Did ya hear what the final challenge is?" Muzo blurted. "We're doing karaoke!"

Karaoke? That came out of nowhere. Unless Thystle had a particular scheme up his sleeve...

The word alone made Poppy whimper in fear. "I can't do it!"

"Aw, come on, Pops, sure you can," Muzo encouraged. "Just belt it out!"

The wolf shifter swayed on his feet like he was about to faint. I put my hand on his shoulder to steady him.

"Poppy, I'm sure you can ask to sit it out," I said gently.

"Yes, especially since the winner of the Games has been chosen," Alaric remarked, his eyes flicking towards me.

Muzo didn't notice. He cocked his head. "Who?"

Poppy released a relieved sigh. "Oh, wonderful. I don't have to sing..."

"Refusing to participate should result in disqualification," Alaric said under his breath, "but it seems the rules in general are looser than I realized."

Whoops. Having sex with Thystle behind the scenes definitely bent the rules, but it was too late to take it back now. Besides, I didn't regret it. The current soreness in my rear end was a pleasant reminder of me and Thystle's beautiful moment.

But there was no malice in Alaric's comment. It seemed more like a private realization, a hopeful comment instead of a chastising one. Would Alaric break the rules to acquire his dragon mate? Honestly, Taylor and I had done the same. Skirting the made-up rules of a TV show to be with your fated mate was an acceptable crime. I fully supported Alaric's future love infractions.

A moment later, Gaius appeared to summon the contestants onto the beach. I heard it before I saw it. The rhythmic thumping of a bass track carried far across the sand. Its fluctuating volume made it clear the AV people were running a sound test. It was kind of nostalgic.

When we arrived at the beach, we saw the imminent musical arena. Two huge speaker sets thudded while kobolds fiddled with the settings. The staff recycled the quiz show stage from yesterday, but gave it a flashy makeover. It didn't resemble a normal karaoke stage in a bar. It was grand and opulent, almost concert-like. Something about it was strangely familiar.

But I didn't dwell on it long. My gaze zoned in on

169

Thystle, who stood next to Gaius in front of the stage. My pulse stuttered as our eyes met. The same fuzzy warmth I'd felt all during last night blossomed in my chest again.

Thystle flashed me a smile. It was innocent enough to pass as a polite TV smile, but *I* knew it was for me alone.

Gaius bounced forward and cleared his throat. He was cheerier than usual, if that was possible. "Welcome everyone to the third challenge of the Dragonfate Games! I'm excited to reveal our final event..." He gestured dramatically to the stage. "Karaoke!"

Poppy trembled like a leaf next to me. Since Muzo and I flanked him, we pressed closer so he wouldn't topple over.

Gaius waved towards Thystle. "As we learned during the quiz show, Thystle hoards music. So, we're putting your musical talent to the ultimate test!"

My heart clambered into my throat. It dawned on me what Thystle wanted.

A private concert from me. From Aquila.

I sucked in a long, slow breath. He catered this challenge towards me with laser precision. He *knew* I could sing everyone else out of the water.

But after a decade of hiding, could I really get on stage and perform the way I used to?

Gaius went on. "Each contestant will take up the mic and sing the song of your choice while we provide the backtrack. Come on, you all know how karaoke works." Gaius winked. "Thystle will watch from the front row. So, let it all out, and have fun!"

Judging by the excited whooping behind me, most of the contestants were eager to try, whether or not they'd be chosen to win. It was a relief that most of my fellow omegas were enjoying their glorified vacation even if they didn't win the dragon's heart.

Alaric's hand shot up.

Gaius nodded. "Go ahead."

"If we'd rather sit the challenge out, will we be disqualified and sent home?" Alaric asked.

I was surprised at his question. Alaric wasn't the type to back down from a fight. Even though he knew he wouldn't win this season of the Games, he wanted to stay and complete the challenges.

But then I noticed Poppy's wide-eyed gaze staring hopefully at the cat shifter. Had Alaric asked the question for Poppy's sake?

"Let's ask the bachelor himself," Gaius suggested. "Thystle, what do you think?"

Thystle stared right into my eyes, as if challenging me. It was almost a threat—*you're not allowed to refuse.*

My dick twitched at Thystle's dominant gaze. At the same time, I swallowed the lump in my throat. Thystle didn't ask me to sing. He demanded it from me.

I didn't know if it was my dick or my brain that took over, but I nodded without thinking.

That satisfied Thystle. The spell over him broke, and he smiled normally.

"We won't force you. Anyone can withdraw from the challenge without penalty," Thystle clarified.

Poppy let out a shaky sigh of relief, slumping against Muzo as if all his bones melted. His friend gave him a supportive pat on the back.

As everyone else took their seats, I stood frozen to the spot. My heart gunned into overdrive. I couldn't tell if I was terrified or excited. Maybe both.

Thystle strode towards me. He caught my wrist and lowered his voice. "Matteo. Tell me how you feel."

"About what?"

His amethyst gaze flickered to the stage, then back at me. "This."

I parted my lips but couldn't find the right words. The inside of my brain was chaos. It felt like a lump of taffy being stretched in every direction.

Thystle captured my hands and held them gently. "You can do it. We both know that. The whole *world* knows that."

I sighed, staring down at the sand. "I don't know how to describe it... It's almost like shifting. Aquila is clawing at the surface. He wants to break free. But Matteo shoves him down every time. It's like we can't coexist without something going wrong."

Thystle frowned. "Why? Because your so-called friends were shitty to you one time?"

"Ouch," I said with a wry smirk. "But... yeah."

Thystle shook his head. "There's no wall between you and Aquila. You want to create music. You also want a family. A mate." He leaned closer so I saw every lilac speck in his mesmerizing eyes. "Your fated mate is standing right in front of you, and my egg is growing inside your belly as we speak."

Heat flooded my cheeks. Did the body mics catch that? If they did, Thystle didn't seem to care. His concern was solely focused on me.

"You will never want for anything, and I will *always* be here for you," Thystle promised in a low growl that sent a shiver down my spine. "So, let Aquila fly free."

My throat thickened with emotion. I took a deep breath.

"All right," I said.

Thystle's eyes flashed. He gave me a quick, fierce hug. I could tell he wanted to cling to me longer, but wrenched himself away and nodded towards the stage.

"Go," he commanded.

I turned to leave, but Muzo had already scampered on

stage and took the mic. It didn't take long for him to launch into a confident yet screechy rendition of "*Party Rock Anthem*" by LMFAO.

"Maybe I'll wait until he's done," I told Thystle with a grin. Raising my fist, I called, "Go, Muzo!"

The jackal shifter happily absorbed the praise like a sponge and sang louder.

Thystle winced at all the wrong notes—which was every single one. He sighed. "I wish you wouldn't wait... But you're a good friend."

I smiled. "Hey, someone has to be."

I bumped my hand against Thystle's, encouraging him to sit with me. He had a special seat in the front, but Alaric had claimed a few seats in the same row for us. We took our spots and watched Muzo's passionate attempt at karaoke. When it was over, he leapt off the stage with an ecstatic expression.

"Did you guys see that? I was awesome, right?" he asked.

"You were quite a sound to behold," Alaric remarked in the most neutral way possible.

On the other hand, Poppy was genuinely awestruck. "Muzo, you were amazing! I didn't know you could sing so well!"

Muzo grinned as he plopped next to him. "I *do* practice in the shower every day."

Poppy nodded. "I can tell!"

I smiled at their wholesome interaction. This is what friendship was supposed to be—supportive and kind. Not how Vani and Keaux treated me that day.

"All right, who's next?" Gaius announced on stage. He gestured to the front row. "Any takers?"

Alaric nudged me with his elbow. "It's your time to shine."

I was surprised at his sudden show of support. "Alaric..."

He rolled his eyes. "What? You think I'm some hater who wants you to fail? Go do your thing."

"Yeah, go Matteo!" Muzo cheered.

Poppy fidgeted in his seat. "I can't wait to hear you!"

Uplifted by their support, I stood and faced the stage. It loomed like a great beast, beckoning me.

I exhaled. The next time I drew a breath, it wasn't as Matteo, but as Aquila.

A trance came over me. It was the same magic that transformed me between man and eagle, but this was an inner shift. I bolted and leapt onto the stage, bypassing the stairs, and grabbed the mic from Gaius. I ran a hand roughly through my hair, ruffling it and letting it fall into Aquila's signature wild style.

I didn't have Aquila's makeup, costume, or musical backup. But I didn't need it. All I required was a willing audience, the microphone in my hand, and the front row gazing supportively up at me.

Especially Thystle. Just like I'd shifted, so did he. He edged forward in his seat, his hopeful amethyst eyes sparkling brighter than any jewel. He looked like a teenager again, the same 17-year-old Thystle fawning over his Aquila poster. He was clearly obsessed, but that obsession was seeded by pure passion and love—the kind only a fated mate could give.

The crowd sensed something had changed. They fell silent and tense in anticipation. As I gazed across the small sea of people, all my performing experience flooded back to me. My senses blasted into overdrive. My blood surged hot. My skin prickled with an electric current. My whole body was a crackling live wire.

"Chromatimaeus Island," I said gruffly into the mic. "Are you ready?"

From the corner of my eye, I saw Gaius and the AV kobolds exchanging a confused glance. I hadn't told them which backtrack I wanted yet.

I didn't need to. One look into Thystle's eyes told me he already knew.

My mate stood and said, "TalonStorm. *Destiny Rises*."

A second later, the drums and bass kicked in. A familiar shiver rippled through my body. As the instrumentals built to the first lyric, I felt high.

Oh, yeah. I missed this feeling.

TWENTY

Thystle

TEN YEARS.

That's how long I waited for this moment.

Matteo, my fated mate, on stage performing his heart out...it was all I'd ever wanted—and now it was finally in my grasp.

As soon as *Destiny Rises* began, I lost all control. I cheered. I screamed. I made so much noise I lost my voice, then I attempted to scream even more. At one point, I got dizzy from exhilaration, so I stared in dead silence, too enraptured by the sway of Aquila's hips to make a peep— though, I got hard as fuck instead.

Not gonna lie, it was a little embarrassing.

But I didn't care. Not while Aquila held eye contact with me during his insane vocal solo. I was painfully in love, and painfully turned on, too. The only thing I looked forward to more than the performance itself was the sex we'd have afterwards.

Speaking of sex, Aquila practically fucked that mic on stage. That was the only way I could describe it. His performance skills were downright erotic. He oozed sex appeal, confidence, and talent. Plus the way he sang himself raw was distinctly similar to his moans and screams in bed. It pleased my possessive dragon soul that I was the only person who knew that secret side of him.

As the song went on, I felt my heart beating faster and my pants growing tighter. Aquila's performance sent me into a frenzy. My last shreds of restraint vanished, and my dragon form burst out of my human body. Thankfully, I had enough control to refrain from crushing any of Matteo's friends in the front row.

But Aquila's set was so enthralling that nobody seemed to care that the bachelor just transformed into a dragon. All of them were spellbound by the star on stage, singing his guts out.

Aquila didn't miss a beat. He was too experienced to be thrown off by my sudden shift. As he met my gaze, fire burned in my belly. The crowd felt nonexistent. He was singing to me. Just me.

Fuck, I wanted to breed him right there on that stage.

Destiny Rises finally reached its conclusion. As Aquila's final note hung in the air and he breathed hard, the entire beach went silent for a couple seconds before exploding into raucous noise. My scales tingled in excitement. All of that cheering was for *my* mate, and he deserved all of it.

Gaius waltzed on stage. Even he looked awed. "Phew, what a performance! What do you think, Thystle? Do we have a challenge winner on our hands?"

I took a few steps towards the stage, lowering my head towards Matteo. He panted, drenched in sweat. He looked utterly delicious like that. I wanted to eat him up.

"Yes," I growled. "And the winner of the Dragonfate Games."

Gaius chuckled. Quietly, he said, "Wow, you launched right into that, huh?" In his louder announcer voice, he added, "And it looks like we have a winner, folks! What a fabulous way to end season two of the Dragonfate Games. Be sure not to miss the closing ceremonies later this evening!"

The closing ceremonies were the last thing on my mind.

As soon as I announced Matteo as the winner, all bets were off. I snatched him off the stage and launched into the air, beating my wings hard. Time sped by in a blur. The next thing I knew, I'd landed with a *thud* in front of my home castle.

"In case you forgot, I can fly, too," Matteo remarked wryly from the safety of my claws.

"Shut up."

I was in such a rush to get inside that my horns nearly broke the front door threshold. Thank Holy Drake the castle was built with our dragon forms in mind, otherwise I would've brought the structure crashing down.

Just as I rounded the corner to slither up the stairs, I ran into Cobalt. What crappy timing. He was probably leaving for his evening walk down to the water.

Not now, I thought with a mental groan. Why did the universe always get in my way when I wanted to breed my mate?

Cobalt's stoic face took on a hint of surprise. His thick brows raised slightly as he eyed Matteo in my grasp.

"Hello," he said, as if this was a normal way to have a conversation.

Matteo waved at my older brother. "Hi."

Cobalt gave him a curt, yet polite nod. "Good to meet you."

"You, too," Matteo agreed.

As wholesome as their interaction was, I groaned impatiently. "Cobalt, we're a little busy here. Can we do the whole meet-the-family thing later?"

Cobalt didn't respond. He scrutinized Matteo's face and nodded solemnly. Then he rolled up his sleeve, revealing his thick forearm dotted with tiny pink scars, and asked, "Is this him?"

A shiver went through me.

"Yes," I said quietly. "This is Aquila. AKA, Matteo. He's the man I told you about ten years ago."

Matteo blushed. "You told your brothers about me?"

Cobalt nodded. "Thystle was ready to break the family rules in order to meet you. Instead, I challenged him. These scars on my arm are proof of that."

Matteo's jaw dropped. "You *fought* your brother so you could see me?" he squawked, sounding both embarrassed and impressed.

"It's fine, it's a dragon thing," I said, waving it off.

"I wanted to test Thystle's will," Cobalt explained. "I did not want him to throw his life away on a whim."

Matteo's brows raised in confused shock.

Cobalt went on. "But if it was for his fated mate... I allowed it."

I grimaced at the memory. "And then five minutes after Cobalt gave me the green light, the twins told me Talon-Storm broke up."

Matteo's face paled. "Oh, gods. I'm sorry, I had no idea," he murmured.

"It wasn't your fault."

A slight smile curled the very corners of Cobalt's mouth. "I am happy to see you two finally united."

That comment warmed me. "Yeah, I meant to introduce Matteo to the family eventually. Just... not right now."

Cobalt nodded—although, to be honest, I wasn't sure if he got the hint—then left.

"He seems nice, if a little odd," Matteo said.

"That about sums him up. Now, where were we?"

I dragged Matteo to my bedroom—and thanked Holy fucking Drake we didn't run into any more family members on the way—then shifted and locked the door.

Before Matteo got a word out, I pinned him to my bed. He was divine. Sweat-damp, tousled hair clung to his forehead. His heady masculine musk was cut by his flaring omega hormones. The intoxicating scents mingled in the air. I drank it in like a drug, letting it scramble my brain.

I crashed our mouths together. The make-out session turned hot and heavy fast. Growls of pleasure slipped out of me as our tongues warred. When we finally parted for breath, we both gasped for air.

Images of Aquila's performance flashed in my mind. Each one was like a direct jolt to my dick.

An idea struck me. I peeled away from Matteo.

"What's wrong?" he asked breathlessly.

"Wait here," I ordered.

I strode over to my sound system. I delicately picked out a vinyl from my collection, put it on the player, and cranked up the volume. As the needle dropped, the opening notes of *Wings of the Sun* enveloped the room.

Matteo's eyes were wide as I resumed my position on top of him.

"Why are you surprised?" I asked with a grin.

His cheeks deepened in color. "I guess I shouldn't be. I've just never fucked with my own music in the background."

"First time for everything."

As the chords progressed, I kissed Matteo savagely. We writhed against the mattress, arching our bodies together. The sound of Matteo's music flooding the room drove me wild. I got fiercely hard hearing both his raw voice in the song, and his pleasured moans below me. My hoard was on blast, and I was making out with my fated mate—it was a dragon's ultimate wet dream.

Suddenly, Matteo put a firm hand to my chest. I paused.

"What's wrong?" I asked.

Matteo's eyes flashed mischievously. "Do you want *him?*"

My heart lurched when I realized what he meant.

"Yes," I blurted out. "I mean, you *are* him, but. Yes. A thousand percent."

He leaned in and spoke roughly against the shell of my ear. "Then get on your knees, alpha."

A ripple of arousal shot through my bloodstream. My heart thrashed in my chest as I threw myself on the floor obediently.

Matteo—or rather, Aquila—took his sweet time standing up from the bed. He was the star, and he was in charge now. I was just an obsessed fan groveling at his feet.

I stared up at him, starstruck. The sudden shift in his demeanor was striking. He felt like a completely different person.

The music dipped into a low, dark chord. Aquila glanced down at me. A shiver seized my spine.

"You want me?" Aquila asked.

I nodded, too awed to speak. From my spot on the floor, he towered over me, tall and imposing and so fucking hot.

"Say it."

It was a demand, but a cool one, like he didn't care if I complied or not. It was sexy as fuck.

"I want you," I choked out. "So, so bad."

He tilted his head, staring me down, then huffed derisively. "I've seen fans want it more."

That sent me into a frenzy. I clawed at his pants in desperation, clinging to his legs like a pathetic freak.

"Please, *please*, let me suck your cock," I begged.

Aquila smirked. "That's much better."

I threw my dragon's dignity out the window. I became something baser, a creature even more primal and crazed —a fanboy.

Grabbing Aquila's belt, I fumbled it free. I was about to toss it aside when he grabbed my chin and forced me to look at him.

"I recognize you're a lust-crazed whore, but do not throw that," he warned. "Put it down nicely."

My entire body melted.

"Yes, sir," I said shakily.

"Good."

My hands trembled like a baby deer as I placed the belt on the floor. Being scolded like that was a freakish turn-on. I wouldn't have let anybody except my fated mate speak to me that way, but when *he* did it, my systems shut down. I was utterly at his mercy.

With the belt safely put aside, I stared up at him, waiting for his next order. But Aquila arched a brow. "Well?"

He sounded bored, like this was for *my* benefit instead of his—and that made my cock throb harder.

It was all an act, of course. I knew Matteo enjoyed this role play, too. That's what made it so hot. Handing over my power and self-respect to my omega mate, and letting me worship him while he treated me like a pathetic grov-eling fan was such a smutty fantasy.

In the background, the music thrummed. The songs on *Wings of the Sun* were not distinct tracks. They melded seamlessly together in one hour-long journey. As the first track flowed into the second, I unzipped Aquila's jeans and pulled them down to expose his tenting briefs. The scents hit me like a slap to the face—the rich, musky scent of cock combined with the addictive perfume of omega. It was all wrapped up together with Matteo's natural, personal scent, and it drove me wild.

I groaned in pleasure, smearing my face against his straining underwear. The sensation of his hard cock pushing into my cheek made my dick throb. I mouthed the shape of his erection through the fabric mindlessly. I felt stupid with lust.

Aquila huffed. A second later, his fingers gripped my hair—firm, but not enough to hurt—and pulled me back.

"Too horny to blow me properly," he remarked. "That's cute."

He angled my head, bringing it towards his cock again. I was close enough to smell, but not touch. The temptation frustrated me. I whimpered like an impatient, untrained dog.

Aquila smirked. "Since you're such a big fan, I suppose I can help you."

My eyes widened in excitement, and I nodded fervently. Whoever said dragons were dignified never met a *really* horny one.

Aquila teased me. He hooked his thumb into his waistband, then lowered it agonizingly slow. It felt like an eternity passed before his hard cock finally popped free of the underwear.

But when it did, the last of my brain cells vanished. All I knew was my mate's cock hanging in front of my face.

I didn't wait to latch on. Matteo's salty, musky flavor exploded on my tongue. As I bobbed my head back and forth, I drooled on his dick. I felt it trickling down the corners of my mouth. I went breathless as I sucked him off. My moans and whines of pleasure were muffled by his fat length. It was an obscene display, but I didn't give a shit. I was literally sucking Aquila's cock. I fantasized about this exact moment a thousand times in my life. Many jerk-off sessions were fueled by the thought of scraping my knees on the ground as Aquila fucked my mouth.

Aquila's hand curled around the back of my skull.

"That's it," he said, his voice hoarse. "Let me use that pretty mouth of yours, dragon."

A burst of arousal hit me like a sledgehammer. I moaned around his cock.

Aquila scoffed in amusement. "You like that?"

I whimpered affirmatively, nodding as best I could.

His fingers clenched my hair harder. My skin sizzled in anticipation. I wanted him to use me, to treat my mouth like a toy.

Aquila drew his hips back, then thrust into my mouth. It was so full that the choked sound that escaped me had nowhere to go.

"Fuck, that's good," he mumbled.

I sat on my knees obediently as Aquila face-fucked me. His pleasured moans layered over his music vocals in the background. I felt like I'd died and gone to heaven.

But I didn't want to come yet. I clamped my fingers around the base of my aching dick, refusing to let my impending orgasm escape. I had special plans for it.

"Fuck, this fanboy's face-hole is hot," Aquila muttered between huffs of breath. "I love using it as my own personal fuck toy..."

My eyes rolled into the back of my head with pleasure. I wanted to moan, but Aquila's cock stretched my mouth and choked me every other second, mangling the sound. My chin was coated in spit and pre-cum. I wanted him to release every single drop down my throat.

He suddenly tensed. Hissing, he grabbed the back of

my head with both hands. The rhythm of his thrusts intensified, pumping faster and harder until his body seized, and he let out a scream that overpowered the music.

His voice was so fucking hot, I nearly came, but clamped down on myself to stop it. It was even more difficult since Aquila emptied himself in my mouth. Hot, thick cum poured down my throat in jets.

I saw stars as he finally pulled away. He braced against the bed and breathed in big, hard gulps.

"Fuck, that was *everything*..." he said, short-winded. Then he grasped my shoulders gently. "Shit, Thystle, are you okay?"

I smirked as I wiped my mouth on the back of my arm. "Oh, don't worry about me. That was only one of the top ten moments of my life."

Matteo exhaled. "You scared me for a second. I thought I'd asphyxiate you by accident."

"I dunno, death by blowing Aquila sounds like a good way to go."

He rolled his eyes, flashing me a grin. "Pervert."

"Yeah. I'm about to be."

As the high of being Aquila's fuck-toy ran out, I slipped right into a second high. My alpha dragon instincts, energized by the little nap, exploded. I snatched Matteo like a predator catching my prey and pinned him to the bed. My raging erection dripped pre-cum all over his belly.

I licked my lips. Now, *that* was a delicious sight. I snaked my hand across Matteo's flat belly, smearing my droplets against his skin. He shuddered beneath me.

"You look divine like this," I growled. My dragon soul lay flush beneath the surface of my human form. Parts of my draconic shift slipped through, like my voice and fangs.

And, of course, the desire to breed my mate.

I lowered my face to kiss the soft skin of Matteo's belly.

"Since I already bred you, my egg is growing here. Soon you'll be swollen with it." I planted another trail of kisses. "But I'm not satisfied with that. I'm going to fuck you senseless. I'm going to breed you, over and over, until your hole is stretched and raw and leaking my cum."

Matteo released a tiny gasp of anticipation. His cheeks flushed a deep color as he nodded.

Another rough growl escaped between my dragon fangs. "When you're pregnant and irresistible, I won't be able to keep my hands off you."

Matteo's mouth curved into a grin. "I don't see a problem with that."

"Good. Because you're *mine*."

I couldn't hold my instincts back any longer. As I leaned forward, I felt my dragon fangs jut to their full length. They itched with the need to pierce my fated mate's skin, to claim him.

Matteo's eyes flashed when he saw them. "Are you going to bite me with those?"

I hesitated. "Is... that okay?"

"Yeah. It's just going to make me hard again."

I heaved a sigh of relief, then laughed. "Oh, no. What a big problem."

Matteo raised a finger to curiously touch the blunt part of my fang. "Is this a dragon thing? Biting your mate?"

"Yes. But it won't hurt," I promised. "I don't know how it works exactly, but it releases a kind of hormone that increases your pleasure."

Matteo nodded. "I figured. I was mostly curious since my animal form doesn't have fangs. They're novel and sexy to me."

I growled as I nuzzled his cheek. "You'd better only find *my* fangs sexy."

Matteo arched a brow as he wrapped his arms around

my neck. "I assumed that was obvious. Now, bite me already."

As he spoke, he wriggled his ass invitingly. He must've felt my cock twitching against his entrance. His hole was slippery with omega slick. I had no trouble angling my hips and pushing the tip of my cock inside him.

I recognized the last song on the album nearing its conclusion. Aquila's voice in the background built, rising higher and higher to a peak I knew was coming. While he sang, I brought my lips to Matteo's neck and inched my cock deeper into his ass. My heart raced. I parted my mouth and readied my hips.

Simultaneously, I bit down on Matteo's neck and buried my cock into him.

Aquila's voice hit a crescendo. Not just in the song, but also straight from my mate's mouth. The mirrored sounds of Matteo's raw, unbridled scream sent me over the edge. I sank my fangs deeper as I came, pleasure exploding in my body's every nerve. I pumped Matteo full of my seed. Wave after wave of hot dragon cum flooded his ass until I was fully spent.

I unhooked my fangs from Matteo's neck. They receded back to normal human teeth. I pulled out of him slowly, both embarrassed and satisfied at the amount of leftover cum that spilled out of him. Mine wasn't the only fluid present, either. Judging by the streaks of white across his belly, Matteo had finished for a second time.

"Might be time to invest in waterproof sheets," Matteo remarked.

I laughed. Even during a moment like this, he was practical. I laid next to him and kissed his cheek.

"You're right," I said. "I love you, by the way."

He blushed, like he hadn't expected that. "I love you, too, Thystle."

I nuzzled closer, purring with giddiness. "I love you the most. Don't fight back."

My mate grinned and stroked my hair. "Fine, but only because you'll bite me if I refuse."

"You liked it."

"I did."

Closing my eyes, I nestled against Matteo. I wanted to be as close as possible to him. He sighed softly as he curled into my chest, and I instinctively put my arms around him. The scent of his sweet breath and warm body allured me.

"Thystle," Matteo said. "Can I ask something about your brother?"

I raised a brow. "Not the post-sex discussion I expected, but sure, go for it."

"Cobalt said something strange earlier," Matteo mused.

I yawned as I pressed my cheek to his. "He says a lot of strange things."

Matteo shook his head thoughtfully. "What did Cobalt mean he said you might 'throw your life away'?"

"Oh. That." I sighed, trying to untangle the family drama in my head. "Remember how I wanted to attend the TalonStorm concert? Well, to do that, I had to leave the island. Since I wasn't an adult yet, I wasn't allowed."

Matteo sounded surprised. "You weren't allowed to leave? But you're dragons. You have wings."

A wry smile quirked the corner of my mouth. As an eagle shifter, Matteo understood the intrinsic urge to fly better than ground-dwelling shifters. One more reason he was my perfect mate.

"Yes. But Cobalt thought that just because we *could* fly, didn't mean we *should*."

Matteo shook his head. "I don't understand. You were almost seventeen. It wasn't like you were an immature fledgling."

I closed my eyes as I nestled against him. "It was Cobalt's way of keeping us safe. Since he's the oldest, he considers it his responsibility." I paused. "And he had a good reason for being cautious. There was an... incident with one of my other brothers."

"What happened?" Matteo asked.

I was quiet for a moment since I didn't know how to explain it, or if I even should. Matteo took my silence as hesitation. He caressed my face softly.

"I don't mean to pry," he said. "If I'm your mate, then we're family. So, I want to know your brothers, too." In a lighter tone, he added, "Maybe once we stop having sex all the time, I can finally meet them."

I chuckled. "Trust me, you will. But less sex isn't an option." I gave him a quick kiss on the lips. "Do you remember the closing ceremonies last season?"

"Yes. You and your brothers were all there."

"Not quite," I corrected. "One was missing. My brother, Viol."

Matteo's brows raised. "I didn't realize. He's not interested in the Games?"

"That's the thing. He *is* interested. At least, he seems to be. But nobody ever really knows what he's thinking, so..." I trailed off with a shrug. "He wasn't always like that. I remember him being nice when I was little. But he left the island as a teenager, and when he came back, he wasn't the same."

"Was he hurt?" Matteo asked, brows knitted in sympathy.

"I don't know," I replied honestly. "He's never told anyone the whole story. All we can do is guess. That's why Cobalt banned the younger dragons from leaving the island without a damn good reason until we were older."

Matteo tapped his forearm, alluding to Cobalt's scars. "And why he challenged you to prove your will?"

"Yes. Even back then, I knew you were mine, even if nobody else believed me."

Matteo blushed, then sighed. "Geez. All because of a TalonStorm concert."

"Hey, it was important to me," I argued, pouting.

He laughed softly and kissed my cheek. "I know. Just think. Now you'll have private concerts with Aquila any time you want, and you don't even have to leave your bedroom."

I grinned. "And I get to suck you off whenever I want? This is paradise."

TWENTY-ONE

Matteo

THE CLOSING CEREMONIES went off without a hitch. Gaius did his hosting duties by cheerfully rounding out the second successful season of the Dragonfate Games. He announced me as the winner, then drummed up interest in season three. As Gaius proclaimed us the fated couple, my fellow contestants-turned-friends all cheered from the front row. Muzo was the loudest, as usual, but Alaric seemed genuinely pleased at my success, and Poppy raised his voice above a whisper, so that was a win in my book.

But there were also a pair of familiar faces who showed up to support us. Taylor and Crimson sneaked into the crowd with Ruby in tow. My heart lifted to see them. It was nice not just to see Taylor, but to see him so happy. There was a light in his eyes that wasn't there before he got together with Crimson.

I breathed a sigh of relief once the ceremony finished. Being in the spotlight was easier as Aquila. I'd have to get used to it after years of hiding myself away in the background.

Another thing I wasn't used to was the swath of friends

who swarmed me. Muzo led the pack, enthusiastic as always.

"Dude, that was awesome! Gaius was all like, 'these two found their fated mates during the Games', and well, *duh,* your performance last night was so cool, of course you won."

Alaric snorted. "You know Matteo didn't win the Games based on his singing talent, right?"

"Yeah, but it still ruled," Muzo pointed out.

Sighing, Alaric turned to me. "Congratulations, Matteo. You deserve it."

Poppy nodded along. "You two are, um, a really cute couple. Is that okay to say?"

"Of course, Poppy," I said. "And thanks, you guys."

Thystle's hand curved around my waist. It was both a silent show of support and a public claim. Now that the Games were over, he could PDA all over me as much as he wanted.

Crimson's familiar voice chimed, "Well, look what the amethyst dragon dragged in. Nice to see you again, Matteo."

Taylor arched a thick brow at his mate. "Did you avoid saying *cat* because of me?"

"I'm trying to be mindful of my language," Crimson confirmed with a grin.

Taylor rolled his eyes playfully, handed Ruby to his father, then gave me a tight hug. The embrace was a pleasant surprise. On season one, I was friendly with Taylor but kept my distance because of my anxieties. Now I knew I was worried for no reason. He and everyone else *wanted* my friendship.

"Glad you came back." As Taylor pulled away, he said, "You were right about your mate being here, after all."

Thystle blinked. "You knew?"

I smiled at him. "I had a feeling. At the end of season one, I told Taylor that my mate was on this island."

A blush bloomed across Thystle's cheeks. He hooked his thumb into the belt loop of my jeans and pulled me closer with a pouty growl. "You never told me that!"

"It never came up."

"You better not have thought it was any of my stupid brothers," Thystle grumbled.

"One of your so-called stupid brothers is right here, you know," Crimson pointed out.

"And?"

Crimson scoffed. "I, for one, am looking forward to Matteo mellowing you out..."

Taylor shot me a lopsided grin. "Welcome to the family, by the way. Putting the lack of legal human marriage aside, I guess this makes us brothers-in-law?"

Something about that felt right. I nodded eagerly. "Yes, I'd like that."

"You like it when it's Taylor," Thystle remarked wryly. "Just wait until you meet the five others on *my* side..."

Gaius swept into the conversation, patting Thystle on the back. "Don't you mean *six* others, my dragon pal?"

Thystle gave him a look. "Gaius, you're a family friend, not one of my literal brothers."

"Your callous nature wounds me," the gryphon shifter said dramatically, clearly not wounded at all.

"Speaking of brothers," Alaric cut in. "Why didn't they show up for the closing ceremonies this time?"

Impatience and disappointment dripped from his voice. He must've waited for an opportunity to scope the remaining bachelors. Unlike the first season, where Gaius summoned them for an appearance, none of them were present this time around.

Gaius nodded sympathetically. "Believe me, my feline

friend, I tried. But rounding up five dragons ranging from *busy* to *ornery* was too difficult."

Thystle snorted. "Jade is busy, and Viol is ornery, but what about the rest?"

Gaius wagged a finger. "You're only half right. Jade was occupied with admin work, but Aurum was actually the ornery one. Viol was straight-up missing. Since only Cobalt and Saffron were available, I chose to forgo the whole thing. Besides, it adds an air of mystery to the show, doesn't it? We'll put their silhouettes on TV." Gaius arced his arm in the air, imitating a flashy banner. "Who's next to find love? Find out on season three of the Dragonfate Games!"

Alaric wasn't done snooping for info. "And what about us?" he asked, arms crossed. "We were given an open invite to return last season. Since we've lost a second time, are we banned from a third chance?"

Muzo and Poppy perked up, like neither of them had considered that.

"Aw, snap," Muzo said, sounding sad. "This is the last time we'll be here?"

Poppy drooped like a wilting flower. "Oh... But I liked seeing my friends and spending time on the beach."

Taylor's eyes flashed. He was fiercely protective of his friends and the mere concept of hurting their feelings wasn't going to fly with him.

Honestly, it bothered me as well. I knew the moment I met Thystle that we were destined to be together, so my fellow "competition" didn't feel like it. They were a source of comfort. If my experience with my former bandmates taught me anything, it was that *real* friends were never threatened by your happiness.

"They should return. I want them to find their fated mates," I stated.

"Me, too," Taylor said firmly. If he was in tiger form, his hackles would've soared like skyscrapers.

Crimson scoffed at the idea. "Of course not. Don't get your stripes in a twist, my love."

Thystle squeezed my shoulder affectionately. "And Matteo, you shouldn't get your feathers ruffled, either." He spoke to Alaric, Muzo and Poppy. "All three of you are welcome to return anytime until you find your mate. If it's one of us, I mean."

Muzo grinned, then glanced over his shoulder. He gestured with his thumb to the group of other contestants who'd apparently forgotten all about the Dragonfate Games and were engaged in a round of beach volleyball.

Gaius swore under his breath. "I *told* them not to play with that AV equipment. Hey, you!"

As Gaius ran off, Muzo asked, "So, what about those guys? They're contestants too, but uh... I dunno if they want to find love that badly."

"Do *you*?" Alaric challenged him.

Muzo blinked like he'd asked a silly question. "Yeah. Who doesn't?"

Alaric deflated, as if that wasn't the answer he expected. "Fair enough."

Thystle raised his chin. "Duke may be the producer, but we dragons get final say in the contestants. Jade won't mind a little wink-nudge to allow you guys on board."

Crimson sighed wistfully. "Oh, the sweet smell of nepotism."

"You say that like it's a good thing," Taylor said with a snort. "But I guess in this case, it is."

"Especially if Jade ends up falling for one of you," Thystle quipped. He seemed intrigued at the thought.

A flash of excitement skittered across Alaric's odd-colored eyes, but he calmed it with a clear of his throat. "That's a nice sentiment. Thank you for clarifying."

Muzo and Poppy both looked happy to be involved.

"Woohoo! Beach round three!" Muzo cried.

Poppy tilted his head, gently eyeing the infant in Crimson's arms. "If it's not too much trouble, maybe we can stay for a little while and say hi to Ruby?"

Ruby's parents beamed at the opportunity to gush about their son.

"Of course," Taylor said fondly.

"Oh, right," I said, placing a hand on my flat stomach. "On the topic of family members, there's a new one in the works."

Thystle choked while everyone else gaped in shock.

"Seriously, Matteo?" Thystle managed between laughs. "That's how you chose to share that you're pregnant?"

I shrugged. "What? There's no point in hiding it."

Out of everybody, Taylor seemed the least surprised. He grinned. "You're right. Especially since you're going to start showing in less than a month."

My brows raised. "That soon?"

Crimson clicked his tongue at Thystle. "You didn't explain anything about dragon pregnancy, did you?"

Thystle rolled his eyes. "Yeah, like I had tons of time between breeding my mate a couple days ago until the Games literally just ended."

"Dragons," Taylor mumbled, then grinned at me. "Congrats, Matteo. I can't wait for our kids to have play dates."

The mental image warmed my heart. "Me, too."

From the corner of my eye, I saw Alaric's gaze flash enviously. I was deeply sympathetic to him. Being single while watching other omegas close to you find their fated mates and start families must've been an awful feeling.

As the groups dispersed and went about their business, I caught up with Alaric before he could slink off.

The cat shifter huffed when I put my hand on his shoulder. "What?"

"Your mate is here, Alaric," I said. "He has to be."

He pulled a face. "I *know* that. I don't need you to tell me."

There was a disconnect between his words and his expression. He sounded nasty, but my reassurance softened the sharp edges in his face. This was his defence mechanism, like blending into the background and disappearing was for me. Or at least, it used to be before Thystle opened me up.

Alaric kept half-heartedly glaring at me. "Well?"

"I just wanted to say, thanks for being my friend during this season," I said. "I appreciated your company."

The guarded veil in his eyes dropped for a second before it flickered back. He grunted, but gave me a wry look. "That's all you wanted to say? The hormones are making you mushy, Matteo."

It was a compliment disguised as a jab. I had a feeling he wanted those exact same mushy pregnancy hormones more than anything.

I grinned. "Thanks, Alaric."

"Now, get out of here before your thirty-second absence causes your dragon boyfriend to explode."

TWENTY-TWO

Thystle

AFTER THE GAMES ended and the hustle-and-bustle of TV production winded down, I took a couple days to recuperate with Matteo. By recuperate, I meant we fucked for hours in my bedroom while blasting his music. And by a couple days, I meant a week.

Thank Holy Drake my room was soundproofed.

I'd lost count of the rounds, but I was sure we'd completed the third that day. Or maybe the fourth.

I sighed contentedly as I cuddled up next to Matteo, inhaling his sweaty post-sex scent like a drug. "That worked up my appetite," I mused. "Want to go hunting?"

A sly grin worked its way across Matteo's face. "If I shifted now, I'd be weighed down by all the cum you just dumped in me."

"Point taken. We'll go hunting in the fridge instead."

We quickly showered before winding down the stairs towards the kitchen. I laced my hand with Matteo's, loathe to be apart from him even by a few inches.

I threw the fridge door open and scanned it. "What are you in the mood for, Matteo? Dinner? Dessert?"

"Maybe we should hold that thought," Matteo said behind me.

"Why?"

When I turned around, I saw why. All six of my brothers were gathered in the kitchen, watching us with various levels of amusement.

"Look who finally showed up," Crimson remarked. Taylor and Ruby weren't with him, so I figured they were having a father-son moment elsewhere.

I raised a brow at Crimson. "Hey, you're not one to talk. After season one, you and Taylor did your fair share of vanishing for...*reasons.*"

Aurum snorted. "We're all adults here. Just say you guys fucked."

Jade loudly cleared his throat to bypass the semantic shenanigans. He wasn't a prude, but he was clearly more interested in Matteo than our banter.

"Nice to finally meet you," Jade said. He strode over to shake Matteo's hand. "And welcome to the Chromatimaeus family."

Matteo blushed. "Thanks for having me."

"I think Thystle is the one *having* you," Aurum said, then ducked when I threw a loaf of bread at him.

Unlike his smart-alec twin, Saffron sighed wistfully. "You guys look so cute together."

Hearing a compliment from one of the twins was a pleasant surprise. I grinned and pulled Matteo closer by the hip.

"Matteo, the one with the yellower hair is Saffron," I explained. "The one with gold hair and the attitude is Aurum."

"Yo," Aurum called from his seat, handling the bread loaf like a football.

I nodded around the room. "You know Crimson and Cobalt already."

Crimson smiled. "Hey."

Cobalt nodded, stoic but polite.

"That's Jade with the glasses." As my gaze skimmed to the final figure, I hesitated to continue. "And...sitting in the back corner is Viol."

Viol barely lifted his head when I addressed him. He was fully clad in black leather as he manspread in his chair a few feet away from everybody else. I hadn't spoken to him once during the Games, so his opinion of Matteo was a mystery to me. But if he had *anything* negative to say about my mate, I couldn't guarantee his safety. It might end in a flat-out brawl.

The kitchen was dead silent. Nobody spoke.

Viol slowly raised his face to look at Matteo. I tensed, bracing myself to jump to his defense.

But Matteo wasn't fazed by Viol's ominous gaze. He smiled and said, "Nice to meet you, Viol. Thystle's told me good things about you."

I heard an audible intake of breath among the room. Meanwhile, I nearly passed out. Why didn't Matteo just say hi and move on?

"Really?" Viol rumbled, his voice edged with disbelief. Or maybe that was my imagination.

But Matteo held fast. "Yes. It's great to meet you, and everybody else."

Viol smirked. Or was it a smile? It was hard to tell with Viol.

"So, you knocked up with Thystle's egg yet?" Viol demanded.

"As a matter of fact, I am," Matteo replied pleasantly, putting a hand over his belly.

I steeled myself for a degrading remark, but one never came. A crescent-moon of a grin sliced Viol's mouth.

"Cute," he said gruffly. "Can't wait to have another niece or nephew."

That was...not the response I expected. But then again, Viol had a bizarre soft spot for babies. He was aggressively kind to Taylor during his delivery—almost *too* kind. He locked everybody out of the room while Taylor was in labor just to keep him comfortable. It backfired when Crimson was caught in the crossfire, but it was the thought that counted.

"I'm inclined to agree with Viol," Jade chimed in. "Welcoming new family members keeps things interesting around here."

"And who doesn't love baby dragons?" Saffron piped up, a dreamy look in his eyes.

Aurum rolled his eyes but said nothing. Whatever secret disagreement they were having, I was glad to stay out of it.

I coughed. "Well, good talk, everyone. Now, can me and Matteo get some alone time to eat lunch?"

"Sure, we'll let you *eat lunch*," Crimson remarked as he turned to leave. "Anyway, I've got a rambunctious dragonet to save his daddy from."

Matteo grinned at me. "Are you going to save me from our baby, too?"

I kissed him on the cheek. "No, because our baby will be better behaved than Crimson's spawn."

Crimson barked out a loud, echoing laugh before he walked out the door. It was an omen of things to come. I had no doubt my comment would bite me in the ass in a few months—literally.

The weather was beautifully sunny, so we took our lunch to go. We put down a picnic blanket and sat beneath the shade of a tropical tree on the beach, its canopy waving lazily in the breeze.

Matteo smoothed his hand over the patchwork quilt. "Did Taylor make this?"

"He did," I confirmed, putting the woven basket between us. "When he was pregnant, he went on a quilting bender. I swear the amount of quilts in the castle outnumber us three-to-one. It's a fucking fabric army."

Matteo chuckled. "That sounds like him. He's not the type who likes to sit around and do nothing."

"Are you?" I asked.

He rocked his head back and forth. "Not when the creative urge strikes."

"Oh no. Have I been distracting you from your creative urges?" I gasped in horror. "Is too much sex the reason you haven't written music?"

He laughed, his eyes sparkling. "How do you know I haven't been?"

"Don't play with my feelings like that," I warned.

Matteo smiled, leaning in to touch our noses. "Come on, Thystle. Would I do that to you?"

My heart raced as I stared into his eyes. Their warm brown depths comforted me.

He was serious.

"You've been writing songs?" I asked, almost scared to hear the answer.

He nodded slowly. "It's the first time I've been inspired in a long while. Thanks to you."

A hopeful feeling swelled in my chest, like a butterfly emerging from its cocoon.

"Me?" I asked.

Matteo chuckled as he captured my hands in his. "Why are you surprised? It's kind of hard *not* to feel inspired when you stare at me like I'm the only thing in the world."

I growled as I pulled his hands closer, rubbing my thumbs across them. "As far as I'm concerned, you are."

"See?"

My inner Aquila fan fidgeted impatiently. "Are you...gonna share it with me?"

"Eventually," Matteo said. "It's still a work-in-progress."

Despite my impatient draconic nature, I was happy to hear it. Knowing Matteo felt comfortable delving back into his craft was more than enough for me.

A familiar call rang out in the sky. We glanced up to see a strangely-dressed gryphon descending towards the beach. Gaius landed with a flourish, shifting to human form and burning our eyes with his neon yellow shirt. But that wasn't his only odd clothing. He wore an oversized postman's shirt on top of it, along with a chest bag.

"Good day, sirs!" he announced. To Matteo, he added, "I hope the dragons have been treating you well, my fellow feathered friend."

"Why are you dressed like it's Halloween?" I asked.

Gaius scoffed as he reached into his bag. "I would never wear something so casual for Halloween. The reason I'm here is because..." He cleared his throat and pulled out a sealed envelope. "You've got mail! Ah, I've always wanted to say that."

I raised a brow. "Winnie sorts through our mail. Why do you have it?"

"Because unlike half of you dragons, I don't hate fun," Gaius said whimsically.

"I don't *hate* fun," I grumbled.

"Who's it for?" Matteo asked.

Striding over to Matteo, Gaius handed him the letter. "For you, in fact."

A sliver of jealousy edged itself into my ribs. "Who's

sending you mail? It better not be some alpha," I growled, leaning closer.

Matteo blinked, turning the envelope over to examine it. "I don't know. There's no return address."

"Fan mail?" Gaius suggested. "You were quite popular with the audience."

Matteo looked confused. "What do you mean?"

"The second season of the Games have aired already," Gaius said.

"What?" I blurted. "It's barely been a week!"

"Duke and Jade partnered with streaming services this time, so it was on demand ASAP," Gaius explained. "It's the most popular show of the year on every platform!"

Matteo's eyes widened. "Wow. I don't know what to say."

"Does that make you nervous?" I asked. When it came to public appearances, he was slowly coming back out of his shell, so I hoped plunging him in the deep end like this didn't unnerve him.

Matteo was quiet for a moment. "No. I'm okay with it." He smiled at me. "Thanks, though."

I rubbed his back for support. "So, what's in the envelope?"

"I guess we'll find out together," Matteo mused.

He opened it meticulously instead of shredding it like a kid on Christmas morning. What he pulled out was a three page, handwritten letter. As soon as Matteo read the first couple lines, he went still.

"What is it?" I asked urgently. If it was some kind of hate mail, I braced myself to rip it out of his hands.

Matteo hesitated, then murmured, "It's from Vani and Keaux."

His ex-bandmates. I curled my lip. "If they've got anything nasty to say—"

Matteo shook his head. "No, it's okay."

"Like, it's *actually* okay, or you're just saying it's okay so I don't bite their heads off?"

He let out a laugh. "Actually okay, but thanks for caring."

The fight drained out of me. If my mate said it was okay, I'd take his word for it.

Matteo went silent. Gaius and I exchanged a glance. There was nothing to do but wait until Matteo finished reading the letter.

After what felt like an eon had passed, Matteo let out a long sigh and put the letter in his lap. When I noticed his eyes were wet, I got worked up.

"What did it say?" I asked, hoping for their sakes that their words didn't hurt him.

Matteo took a few moments to reply. Finally, he blinked away the tears and said, "They apologized to me."

"Really?"

He gazed down at the letter meaningfully. "I don't know how much of our conversation they aired on the show, but it must've been enough to change their perspectives. They said they didn't realize how much they'd hurt me back then."

"What about the article Talon was talking about?"

Matteo shook his head. "They saw that, too. The whole thing was on air. They said it wasn't true. Vani and Keaux are starting a new project, and they mentioned TalonStorm's break up, but they didn't actually say anything negative about me. The tabloids put words in their mouths and blew it out of proportion. Talon just ran with it."

"Asshole," I growled. "I wished I'd booted him off the island earlier."

Matteo smiled. "You know? I'm glad you didn't. If you

did, the truth might've stayed hidden. It had to get ugly before it got better."

Grumbling, I pulled Matteo closer. "I guess. Still doesn't change the fact that he's a dickhead."

He rested his head on my shoulder. "That we can agree on."

"So, are you going to contact them?" I asked.

"I want to. It's honestly a weight off my chest that there's no bad blood between us," he said. "But the envelope had no return address. Maybe they were nervous I'd take the letter poorly?"

I waved a hand. "Oh, you don't need to worry about that. We're rich dragons, remember? We have ways of finding people."

Matteo grinned. "Aw, how sweet and creepy."

"Hey, it's for love, so it's automatically not creepy."

He chuckled. "Somehow, that makes it sound even creepier."

I rolled my eyes and kissed him, dismissing the half-baked argument.

TWENTY-THREE

Matteo

———————

IT TURNED out Taylor wasn't lying about the accelerated pregnancy. Within three weeks, I was swollen all over and my back killed me.

Thystle suggested talking to Taylor about it, since he was previously the only omega on the island. As much as my mate wanted to help, he was an alpha with no experience being pregnant, and he wanted me to have the smoothest journey possible. He helped out in other ways, of course, but discussing pregnancy with my fellow omega friend was priceless.

We met in the living room—well, *one* of the living rooms in the sprawling dragon castle. This one was thoroughly baby-proofed so Ruby could crawl and explore to his heart's content without adults worrying about him. He tested out his stubby human limbs on the rug.

Thystle joined us, since he never let me out of his sight except to go to the bathroom—and even then, he lurked outside the door 'just in case' I needed help. It was honestly quite sweet.

"So, being pregnant, huh?" Taylor began in his matter-of-fact tone. "How do you feel about it so far?"

I glanced down at my curved belly. It happened so fast that it felt surreal.

"Fine," I said honestly.

"Fine?" Thystle echoed beside me with a slight frown. "You don't feel glowing and radiant and sexy?"

I grinned at him. "Sorry, it's kind of hard to feel radiant and sexy with a beach-ball sized egg inside you."

His eyes glinted mischievously. "Clearly I need to do a better job convincing you..."

"Can we save the flirting for later?" Taylor deadpanned. "This is a serious conversation."

"Very serious. Utmost seriousness," I agreed with a nod.

Taylor arched a brow. "Are you making fun of me while I give you advice?"

"I'd never dream of it."

Before Taylor could respond, Ruby blew a big raspberry, robbing any last scraps of seriousness from the room. I chuckled as Taylor pulled his son into his lap.

"This here is a baby," Taylor stated. "This is the end result of your hard work growing an egg inside you, then laying and incubating it."

I couldn't help but grin. "Taylor, you know I'm an eagle shifter, right? This comes naturally to me."

He almost seemed disappointed that he didn't get to talk about it more. "Then why did Thystle beg me to talk to you?"

I turned to look at my mate. "You *begged* him?"

"No? Maybe?" Thystle squeaked.

Overcome with fondness for my mate, I chuckled and kissed him on the cheek. "Thanks."

Thystle blushed. "You're welcome?"

I made a surprised sound as a sudden weight flopped

into my lap. I glanced down to see Ruby using me as a jungle gym.

"Well, hello there," I said, smiling at the infant. With his unusual striped hair, he was a sight to behold. It made me wonder what my future child would look like.

He made a growly noise akin to a dragon's roar, although with his tiny size it was more of a kitten's mewl, and he sank his half-grown teeth into my arm.

Taylor sighed as he pried his baby off. "Dragonets..."

When Ruby was safely contained in his dad's lap, Taylor grabbed the bumpy pink soother off the coffee table and guided it to his son's mouth. Ruby was happy to chomp on the soft plastic instead of my flesh.

"Gotta love them, though," Taylor added fondly. His eyes flooded with warmth as he watched Ruby gnaw on the toy. "There's nothing like having your own."

A wellspring of feeling overflowed in my chest. Seeing the bond between parent and child fuelled my already raging hormones, the need to love and protect my unborn baby. I ran my hands over my belly, my heart skipping with excitement to meet the child who would hatch from it.

A couple weeks later, the nesting urge started.

Actually, *started* may have been an understatement. It hit me like a freight truck. I woke up one morning and it was all I could think about. Eating, drinking, sleeping... none of that mattered while I began my nest preparations.

"Rooftop," I said suddenly, sitting upright in bed. "Does the castle have a rooftop?"

Thystle made a half-baked, sleepy noise next to me. "Huh?"

My skin felt itchy. Impatient.

"I have to go higher," I muttered.

He blearily turned towards me and blinked. "What're you talking about?"

There was no time to explain. I snatched the blanket off the bed while Thystle was still in it, then ran out of the room. I heard him sputter in confusion.

"Wait, Matteo, where are you going?" he asked.

I wanted to tell him how I felt, but I was choked by the need to nest. The urge was similar to a strike of musical inspiration. When that happened, I couldn't breathe until I got the lyrics and chords down. This was the same, except I needed to gather and arrange nesting materials.

I bolted towards the staircase. One of them went higher, didn't it? I needed access to the roof. If I couldn't take the stairs, I'd go outside, shift, and fly up, but carrying things was easier in human form.

"Matteo, wait for me!" Thystle called down the hall.

I heard his voice and footsteps as he tried to catch up, but I couldn't stop to explain. The urge overwhelmed me. I knew instinctively that I was on a strict time limit.

Clutching the blanket, I ran up the stairs. My skin prickled with sweat and urgency. When I reached the landing, a dark door stood before me.

That must be the exit to the roof, I thought eagerly.

I grabbed the handle—and found it locked. My heart dropped. I came all this way for nothing, and I was running out of time.

The door flew open from the inside. Viol glowered threateningly in the threshold until he saw me. The simmering rage vanished from his expression.

"What are you doing here?" Viol asked.

Sweat dripped from my brow—not because I was scared of him, but because I needed to nest ASAP.

"Rooftop," I managed.

His dark eyes flashed with understanding. Viol didn't waste time. In a blur of iridescence, he shifted to dragon form. It happened so fast, I barely saw it. In the following seconds, he grasped me gently with his paw, then threw himself over the railing. The castle accommodated dragon forms, but Viol flew so fast and erratically, I was afraid he'd tear the whole place down by accident.

During the chaos, I heard Thystle cry out to me, but the rushing wind in my ears smothered his words.

Viol banked his wings when we hit the main floor, sped through the doors, then arched over the building. A couple seconds later, he placed me—and my blanket—down on the rooftop.

"This what you wanted?" he asked gruffly.

I got to work nesting straight away, so I couldn't speak. I hoped my appreciative nod was enough to convey my gratitude.

"Viol!"

Thystle's furious dragon voice ripped through the air like thunder. It startled me so badly that I momentarily forgot about my nest as I whipped around to look at him. A chill ran down my spine when I saw my mate advance on Viol. The two purple dragons faced off, hissing and snarling at each other. Viol was bigger and darker, but Thystle's anger at the perceived injustice flared around his body like a nasty miasma.

"What did you do to my mate?" Thystle snapped, his voice crueller than I'd ever heard it.

Viol didn't respond. He glared him down like he was two seconds away from losing control.

My heart leapt into my throat. I had to intervene before either of them got hurt.

I dropped the blanket and ran between them. I hugged one of Thystle's front arm to grab his attention.

"Wait, Thystle," I cried. "It's okay. He didn't hurt me. He just brought me to the rooftop like I asked."

The muscles beneath Thystle's scales relaxed, and the

vicious growl in his throat subsided, but he didn't change back to human form. He lowered his scaly maw to nuzzle me.

"Do you know how worried I was?" he asked in his gravelly dragon voice.

I stroked the side of his face. "I know, I'm sorry. But Viol was only helping, so please don't bite his face off."

Viol scoffed, flicking his tail dismissively as he turned around. "He could *try*."

Thystle narrowed his eyes, but I drew his attention back to me by kissing the front of his snout. That was enough to diffuse his well-meaning alpha overreaction.

"Fine," Thystle muttered. "Next time, just talk to me. I would've been happy to fly you to the roof."

He liked the kiss, so I gave him another one. "I promise, I will. Now, I *really* have to make my nest."

"Can I help?" Thystle asked.

"You can stand there and look sexy."

"Done."

As I hurried to pick up the blanket, the instincts flooded back in full force. Now that the immediate threat was done, I could concentrate on nesting. But it quickly became apparent that a single blanket wasn't enough. I fussed with the blanket over and over, unable to find the best configuration.

Frustration crept over me. I didn't have much longer, but I couldn't bring my egg into this world without the perfect nest. My eagle soul wouldn't allow it.

Thystle must've sensed my annoyance. He touched his wing-tip to my shoulder. "Are you okay?"

"No," I said curtly. "I need more materials."

"I can get more," Thystle offered.

The thought of him abandoning me right now was too much. I shook my head. "No. Please, stay here."

I knew I was acting crazy, but I couldn't help it. My hormones and instincts raged out of control. All I wanted was the best for my egg, and I wanted it *now*. Was that too much to ask?

Thystle's scaly brow furrowed in concern. He was quiet as he mulled over the options. "We could—"

Saffron's sudden muffled voice cut him off, yelling, "We came as fast as we could!"

A rainbow of dragons landed on the rooftop. My eyes widened as Thystle's brothers circled us. Each dragon carried a mouthful of nesting materials, from blankets, to dry straw, to driftwood.

Jade placed his neatly folded blankets by my feet. "We heard you were in need of assistance."

Crimson added a few handmade quilts to the pile, courtesy of Taylor. "Why didn't you say so earlier? It would've saved us a lot of commotion."

Even Thystle seemed awed by his brothers' rush to help. "Where did you guys come from?" he asked.

Saffron deposited his intriguingly-shaped driftwood before me. "Viol told us," he explained.

Aurum snorted and dropped a clump of straw beside his twin's offering. "More like *screamed*," he mumbled. "It felt like he'd kill us if we didn't bring you nesting materials ASAP."

"I would," Viol said darkly.

Aurum yelped in shock, his eyes going wide as plates as he flattened to the ground. Viol had manifested behind him like smoke, glaring at the golden twin in a clear order to shut the hell up.

I took Aurum's offering with a smile, hoping to dispel Viol's murderous energy. "Thank you, everyone. This is exactly what I wanted."

Apparently satisfied by this, Viol reined in his dark aura. Aurum sighed in relief.

Cobalt seemed oblivious to the drama beside him. He nudged a large rock towards the pile. "For your nest. I hope it helps."

"Dude, it's a rock," Aurum said. "How is that comfortable?"

Cobalt's shoulders drooped. "Golden eagles nest on cliffs. I thought he would like it."

My heart squeezed with affection. Thystle's whole family jumped to my aid without a second thought. I couldn't have been happier.

I grabbed the rock and rolled it into the nest. It sat on top of the blankets and straw, holding everything nicely in place. Cobalt was right. The addition of the rock sparked my eagle instincts. I felt soothed by its presence as I sank down into the nest.

"It's perfect, Cobalt," I said. "Thanks."

The massive blue dragon perked up, pleased.

Thystle made that growl-purr sound that vibrated in his throat. "Feeling better?" he asked, nuzzling my cheek.

"Much," I said with a content sigh.

Jade smiled. "Glad to hear it. Remember, Matteo, you're part of our family now. If you ever need help, you simply have to ask."

My chest swelled with feeling. "I will. Thanks, Jade." The warm fuzzies were interrupted as a sudden cramp in my side made me wince. "Ow."

"Sounds like contraction o'clock," Crimson commented. "Let's leave these two to their egg-laying, shall we?"

The dragon brothers wished me well before taking flight to give us privacy.

Well, all except one.

Viol lurked at the far end of the rooftop, glowering in our direction. He seemed reluctant to leave.

Thystle pulled away from me.

"You're not starting anything with him, are you?" I asked.

"No," he promised.

My mate approached his brother. The two dragons stared at each other, neither one wanting to back down.

But why didn't Viol want to? I wasn't his mate, and I felt no romantic feelings from him. The concern he showed was purely platonic. Was he just worried about me?

"Viol," Thystle growled in a neutral tone. "I've got this. You can leave."

Viol slowly flicked his tail. "You sure?" he challenged.

"Matteo is my mate. He's my responsibility, not yours."

"A pregnant omega is *all* of our responsibility," Viol countered. There was no vitriol in his voice. He spoke as if stating a fact.

His comment didn't really surprise me. During our first family meeting in the kitchen, he came across as gruff but well-meaning, especially towards children. That confirmed my hunch that he only had my best interest in mind when he'd snatched me away.

Thystle took a breath. "I appreciate your help. Without you, Matteo wouldn't have the nesting materials he needed. So, thanks. But I'll take it from here."

Viol's dark gaze slid towards me. When I nodded, he blew out a puff of smoke. "Fine. Good luck," he added genuinely.

Then he unfurled his wings with a *crack* and took to the sky, disappearing into the island mountains.

Thystle returned to my side, curling around me and my

nest. "Sorry about the family drama," he mumbled. "I know they can be a lot sometimes."

I stroked his side. "Don't worry about it. I like having a big, new family. And I don't know why you were so nervous about Viol. He's not that bad."

Thystle snorted. "Saying Viol isn't that bad is like comparing a puppy to a tarantula. Enough about him. How are you?"

I wiped the sweat off my brow. "Fine. Definitely about to lay an egg."

"I'm here," Thystle murmured, rubbing his face against my neck. I could tell he wanted to be as close as possible to soothe me, which was sweet. Plus, the coolness of his scales was a welcome distraction.

A throb of pain coursed through my lower body. I was glad to be sitting already, otherwise my knees would've failed me. I hissed and curled my fingers against Thystle's side. I appreciated his support—both emotional and physical.

"Clothes," I managed through my teeth.

The agony robbed me of the ability to string more than two words together, but thankfully, Thystle understood. He craned his neck so his maw was above my pants. There was no way he could tug them off without shredding them, but that was fine with me. Pants were replaceable.

Thystle's fangs made quick work of the obstructing clothes. Once my pants transformed into a pile of fabric scraps, I sighed in relief. With my lower body free, I could finally put in the real work of birthing my egg. I knew it wouldn't be long now.

My eagle instincts took over. Closing my eyes, I concentrated on the sensation of the egg, how desperately it wanted to be free. Sweat prickled my skin as I focused. I threw my weight into Thystle, bracing myself against him as I pushed harder.

"You're doing great, Matteo," Thystle purr-growled in my ear.

That little encouragement gave me the final burst of strength I needed. With a gasp, I felt a weight literally lifted from my body.

But there was no time for relief. I bolted upright, staring into the nest, eager to see my egg.

And when I did, my eyes widened.

What I'd birthed was no regular bird egg. For one thing, it radiated a purple shine like a glow stick. I expected a creamy-white shell—instead, the egg looked like it was carved from a chunk of amethyst. I laid my hands on it, surprised at its smoothness and warmth. I couldn't help but smile in disbelief at the way the glow disappeared beneath my hands, then shone through my fingers as I parted them.

"Thystle, this is incredible," I murmured. "Are all dragon eggs like this?"

"I've only seen two," Thystle answered. "Ours, plus Taylor and Crimson's egg. Theirs glowed red. So far, it's two for two lava lamp babies."

I snorted at the term, then pulled the egg into my lap. "Lava lamps aren't the first thing I think of. It reminds me more of those glowing Himalayan salt lamps."

"Himalayan, what now?"

I grinned. "How do you know what a lava lamp is and not a salt lamp?"

"Sorry I can't keep up with every human contraption," Thystle mumbled. "It's not my fault they think of new crap every day."

I chuckled and patted his neck. "You're right. It's a lot to keep up with. Never mind that. Look at our egg."

"I haven't stopped staring since you laid it," Thystle

replied, arching his neck so he could be closer. "How can I when it's so beautiful?"

He was right. I'd never laid eyes on anything as gorgeous as our egg. It literally looked like a piece of art. But more than its physical beauty, my heart brimmed with happiness knowing our baby grew inside that glittering purple shell.

"How long will it take to hatch?" I asked my mate, eager to meet our child.

"Ruby took about a month," he said warmly. Nuzzling my cheek, he added, "It won't take long, Matteo. So, let's enjoy our egg while we can before it hatches into a crawling bitey gremlin."

I grinned. "I'm looking forward to that."

TWENTY-FOUR

Thystle

HOLDING a sushi tray in one hand, I huffed and puffed up the stairs. I wasn't out of shape by any means, but climbing the stairs to the roof while carrying a huge tray of sashimi and maki rolls was enough exercise to break a sweat.

Matteo told me half an hour ago he'd craved sushi, so I had the chefs whip it up for him. I genuinely loved catering to his every whim. It satisfied my alpha instincts to nurture and protect him, even if it meant running to the kitchen every thirty minutes to sate his cravings, although he'd laid his egg and wasn't pregnant anymore. He was now in the brooding stage. Not *brooding* as in me when I got moody, but literally bird-sitting-on-an-egg brooding.

Since he built his nest on the rooftop, he wasn't eager to move it. That was fine by me. We set up a temporary office for him on the roof, complete with a wide weatherproof canopy, cozy pillows, and a microphone and laptop to work. I offered more, like a stereo system and TV, but Matteo was a simple man who didn't ask for much.

Well, except sushi trays. I was more than happy to arrange those.

I grunted as I finally lugged over the last step. I wiped the sweat from my brow and called, "Hey, Matteo."

He didn't respond. He sat with his back to me, typing frantically on his keyboard. I couldn't see it from my angle, but I knew our egg was curled up safe and warm in his lap.

But it worried me when Matteo didn't respond. He was usually ecstatic to receive his treats, greeting me with a kiss and a smile. This time, he didn't even acknowledge me. I wanted my kiss and smile, dammit.

"Matteo, are you okay?" I asked, walking closer.

He perked up visibly at the sound of my voice, but still sounded distracted when he called back, "Yeah, one sec."

I raised a brow. What could possibly be more interesting than his alpha mate arriving with a tray of sushi?

"You'd better not be chatting with alpha dragon singles in your area," I teased as I stood behind him.

I was obviously joking, but the way he slammed his laptop shut made me raise a brow.

Matteo huffed. "I was doing something private," he said mildly.

"You're on an open rooftop," I reminded him. "So, *were* you chatting with hot dragon singles in your area?"

Matteo rolled his eyes as he stood up. Our egg glowed brightly, painting his arms and chest in a diffused purple light. He smiled as he leaned in and captured my lips in a long, passionate kiss. The sizzling make-out stomped out my tiny worm of jealousy.

"You think that little of me?" Matteo murmured with a grin. "I have *you*, Thystle. You're my alpha, the father of my baby, and my number one fan. Nobody else could ever compare."

Warm happiness bubbled in my chest. I leaned over the sushi tray to kiss him again. When I pulled back, I asked,

"What's with the secrecy, then? I feel left out. And I even brought you sushi," I added, pouting for good measure.

Matteo grinned sympathetically. "I know dragons are impatient, but just wait a little bit, okay? I promise, it'll be worth it."

"Fine," I said. "But in exchange for being patient, you'll let me feed you sushi."

"How is that a trade? Those are both wins for me."

I scoffed. "Are you kidding? Feeding our mates is a hardwired sexy activity for us dragons. It's basically foreplay."

Matteo arched a brow. "Is that a promise?"

"Obviously. Now, sit."

Matteo sat, keeping our egg huddled in his lap. His weird quilt-and-rock nest was odd, but if he was comfortable, that was all that mattered. I took a careful seat beside Cobalt's rock so it didn't jab into me, then pulled the lid off the tray and pulled out the ceramic chopsticks.

I picked up a piece of tuna maki and offered it to Matteo. "Say *ahh*."

"Are you practising for when the egg hatches?" he teased.

"I might be. Hurry up and eat it so I can feed you another one."

Grinning, Matteo ate the roll and let out a satisfied sigh. "Mm, that's good. Give that chef a raise."

"Done," I promised, then picked up a thick slice of salmon sashimi. "I bet the sushi wasn't this good when you lived in human society, huh?"

"Nope." As he swallowed the sashimi, I watched it slide down his throat like a pervert. The visual filled my mind with dirty ideas. I picked up a second slice and thrust it at him.

Matteo chuckled. "At the rate you're feeding me, I'm going to gain thirty pounds."

"Don't threaten me with a good time."

He rolled his eyes, not believing me. "I'd lose my rock-star bod." He glanced down at himself. "Although now that I'm over thirty, I'm already getting there."

I scowled. No way in hell was I going to let my mate feel self-conscious over his body.

"I don't give a fuck if your body changes, Matteo," I growled. "You're hot, and you're *mine*, no matter what you look like."

He blushed, his mouth curving into a smile. "Thank you, Thystle."

"You're welcome. Now, eat."

After we polished off the tray together, Matteo leaned against my shoulder. Our egg glowed like a purple night-light. I stroked its smooth shell, feeling paternal instincts flare up within me.

"It's been a whole month since you laid it," I murmured, running my thumb along the faceted shell.

"Any day now, huh?" Matteo suddenly sat up and opened his laptop. "Oh, that reminds me. I've talked to Vani and Keaux since they sent me that letter."

Curious about his screen, I leaned over, but Matteo turned it away. I frowned like a grump.

"Patience," Matteo chided.

"I hate patience," I mumbled.

"I'm aware."

I dutifully kept my eyes averted from the screen. "I'm glad you guys reconnected, but what does the day have anything to do with them?"

He tapped away on the keyboards. "Back during our TalonStorm days, we'd give each other deadlines. You know, shared responsibility type of thing. It was easier to keep each other in check than have the label breathing down our necks."

"Still not following," I said.

"V and K are hounding me, since today's my deadline for...something."

I pursed my lips like I'd sucked a lemon. "I hate patience *and* secrets."

Matteo sighed. He purposely pulled away from the laptop and smiled as he put his hand on top of mine. "There's no secrets between us. Think of it more as a surprise. But if you really want me to tell you, I will."

My curiosity smothered my impatience. "A surprise? For who?" I asked.

"For *you*. Who else?" Matteo said, like it was obvious.

I blushed, embarrassed I'd made such a big deal about it. "Oh. I can wait."

He looked pleased as he returned to his laptop. "Great. It'll be worth it. I hope."

"Well, are you done whatever it is?" I asked, still moping. I selfishly wanted Matteo's undivided attention, which I couldn't get if he was chatting with his friends.

His hands flew over the keys, then he hit a button with gusto, blowing out a loud exhale. "There. Done." He shut the laptop and turned to me with a grin. "Now, I'm all yours."

I angled my mouth against his and gently nipped his lower lip. "You're *always* all mine," I reminded him.

He made a soft pleasured sound. "Mm. About that foreplay you mentioned..."

I licked my lips, instantly aroused. I put my hands on his shoulders, ready to push him to the ground and straddle him when I heard a small *crack*.

"What was that?" Matteo asked.

When I glanced down at the egg, my eyes went wide as plates. A tiny hole appeared at the top of the shell.

"It's hatching," I blurted out. "Holy shit, Matteo, our egg is hatching!"

He grabbed my arm, digging his fingers into my skin hard with excitement. He went quiet as his instincts took hold of him. His sole focus was on our egg, making sure it hatched properly.

The egg wriggled, then lurched sideways. If it wasn't safely nestled in Matteo's lap, it would've rolled across the rooftop. A second later, a second hole pipped in the shell. It was followed by a distinctive dragonet squeak. The sound of it made my heart soar. Our baby fought hard to escape its eggy prison, and knowing its parents, it was stubborn as hell.

There was a second of silence before a huge chunk went flying out of the nest. It left a big hole behind, accompanied by a baby dragon foot. It was literally kicking its way out of the egg.

"It's coming," Matteo breathed, still grasping my arm for dear life.

I nodded. "Any second now..."

Another big crack. The remaining shell walls crumpled as the baby dragon's head jutted out of its egg, letting out a triumphant squeak of freedom.

The dragonet had pale purple scales, like lilac blossoms in spring, and they had Matteo's gorgeous deep brown eyes. Their short limbs were chubby and adorable.

Matteo pulled the baby loose from the egg, then his animal side overwhelmed him. He shifted to eagle form and settled his soft feathers on top of the baby to keep them warm.

Unfortunately for my poor mate, our baby wasn't having it. I laughed as the dragonet chirped and thrashed, tossing Matteo aside like he was an annoying hat instead of his dad.

"Sorry, Matteo," I said. "Dragonets don't like being sat on."

My mate's chest feathers puffed up. "I wasn't sitting, I was brooding..."

I grinned at the irony of that particular word. But despite being scorned a second earlier, the baby dragon crawled towards Matteo, pressing close to his downy feathers. Matteo settled contentedly. He sank into the nest and draped his wing over the baby's side.

My heart squeezed with affection. I sat next to Matteo, stroking his back. Even as a bird, it wasn't hard to tell he radiated joy.

He chirped, gently nuzzling our baby with his beak. The dragonet responded with a growly chirp of their own. I could've died of cuteness overload.

"You're perfect," I said. "You and Heather both."

We'd chosen the name together, inspired by the rustic purple flowers. We figured our baby would have purple scales like me, and the wildflowers also reflected Matteo's down-to-earth nature. Although humans used it as a feminine name, we both thought of flowers as being gender neutral, and since our child would be raised away from human society, there was no risk of being teased no matter what gender they ended up being.

Matteo beamed at me proudly. "You're pretty perfect, too."

I grinned before planting a kiss on his feathery head. "Then we're a perfect little family."

Heather yawned, then pawed at Matteo's side demandingly. They clearly thought it was feeding time.

"Dragonets can eat solid food right away, right? Too bad we just finished off the sushi tray," Matteo mused.

"Hey, it's never too late for more sushi." I scooped up Heather in my arms. "Are you ready for your first ever sashimi dinner, little one?"

Heather yowled in agreement, their sharp rows of tiny teeth demanding flesh.

I laughed. "Then off to the kitchen we go."

TWENTY-FIVE

Matteo
———————

AS I CHECKED MY WATCH, my heart thumped with nervous excitement. It was almost time for the big surprise I'd planned for weeks now. Gaius waited for me on the beach, and we still needed to go over a couple logistics before the whole thing unfolded.

But to do that, I had to sneak away from Thystle, and that was a big problem. He preferred to be glued together for all time.

"Hey, Thystle," I said, slipping off the bed. "Do you mind watching Heather for a while?"

He nodded, taking the plump infant without question. He grinned as our dragonet wriggled like an overgrown lizard in his lap, flailing their tiny claws until Thystle produced their chewed-up teething ring. Heather clamped on the soother like a crocodile chomping its prey.

"Where are you going?" Thystle asked casually.

I was already in the doorway when I answered, "Somewhere."

He raised a brow. "Very descriptive. Are you escaping from me, or from Heather?"

Heather spat out the teething ring on cue. Thystle

pulled out a second chew toy from his fanny pack. He normally wouldn't be caught dead wearing one, but for Heather, he made every exception in the book. Heather happily went back to gnawing on the soft plastic.

I chuckled. "I'm not escaping from either of you. You know I *always* want to be with you two."

Thystle snorted, still sounding playful. "Apparently not."

I doubled back to where Thystle sat on the bed and gave him a long, reassuring kiss.

"If you really must know, it's part of your surprise," I murmured. "So, can you be a good little fanboy and sit here patiently for an hour?"

He blushed at being called a *good little fanboy*, then nodded.

"I'll send someone to get you in an hour," I promised. "Oh, and keep those blinds closed. No peeking through the window."

Thystle slowly turned towards the window, like he hadn't realized that was an option.

I clicked my tongue. "Ah, ah."

Thystle groaned. "Fine."

He slumped into bed, pulling Heather along with him. They giggled and started using Thystle's body as a playground. I laughed at the sight of an oblivious bubbly Heather clambering over Thystle's pouty face.

"It won't be long," I promised. "And you'll love it. I hope."

The corner of his mouth pulled into a wry smile. "I will. Don't worry. Get out of here already, before I get impatient and break the rules."

I caught up with Gaius on the beach. The sight of the gryphon shifter—and what he'd set up behind him—filled me with instant relief. For all of Gaius's whimsy and quirky passion for eye-searing shirts, he was solidly reliable.

As I got closer, my jaw dropped. I stumbled to a halt and stared. The stage was twice as extravagant as it was during the Games. There were bigger speakers, a light display, and even a fog machine to create a moody atmosphere. A drum set and an electric guitar stand flanked a single microphone in the center of the stage.

My microphone.

A shudder chilled my spine. This familiar scene brought back so many memories—most of them great, some not so good. But those old tainted memories were changing, too. I'd since made up with Vani and Keaux after a few long talks over the phone. We each apologized for the way we handled the messy misunderstanding, and the fallout that came after it. Now that we were all in our thirties, it was embarrassing to look back on the way we acted a decade ago.

Vani and Keaux took their apology a step further. Our big argument was about me finding a mate and settling down. It turned out that after TalonStorm's dissolution, Vani and Keaux got together after frustrating years of mutual pining. Who would've thought?

A hand landed on my shoulder, pulling me back to the present.

"Looking good so far?" Gaius asked with a grin.

"Everything's perfect," I said. "Thanks again for all your help. I wouldn't have been able to do this without you."

He winked. "Anything for a feathered friend. Oh, and a dragon, too, I guess."

"What's this about dragons?" Jade asked, poking his head into the conversation.

Gaius stood up straighter. "Nothing, dear dragon of mine."

Jade's green eyes sparkled with amusement. He was clearly poking fun at the gryphon. He turned to me and asked, "Are you ready, Matteo?"

I blew out a breath. "Getting there."

Jade nodded in understanding. "Karaoke aside, it's been a long time since you performed."

Crimson strolled by, joined by Taylor and Ruby. "Especially with your backup," he added.

I grinned. "Crimson, they're not backup, they're the other two-thirds of the band."

"Psh," he said, waving a dismissive hand.

Taylor nudged his mate. "Don't say that so loud. You're going to give the humans a bad impression."

"What do I care about a human's opinion?" Crimson asked with a haughty sniff.

I smiled. I knew Crimson's attitude came less from his dislike of humans, and more from his desire to protect me. It didn't matter to Thystle's brothers that I only recently joined the family. They all treated me like I'd been part of it forever. It was a warm, welcoming feeling.

"I know they're humans, but they're my friends," I explained.

Jade gave Crimson a pointed look behind his glasses. "Yes, and we made special arrangements to have them here for one night only. I expect you can behave for a few hours, yes?"

"Yes, yes," Crimson replied, only to be elbowed by Taylor again. "Ow."

"Did you say *humans*? Where?"

"We want to see them!"

The pair of voices could only belong to the twins. They manifested side-by-side like a pair of horror movie characters in a hallway, except they were eagerly looking around for any sign of humans.

"Don't freak them out," Crimson said. "Otherwise they'll go back to their human world and tell everyone how terrifying dragons are." He paused. "On second thought, go ahead and freak them out."

"Crimson," Taylor said in a fond warning.

"Fine, I'm behaving."

Since the whole family was invited to the show, I looked around for the remaining two dragons.

"Where's Cobalt and Viol?" I asked.

Aurum cocked his head towards the water. "Cobalt's over there staring at the sea. He seemed excited about the show, so I think he just got distracted. Dunno if Viol will come, though."

"Yeah, he heard humans were gonna be here, and noped out of it," Saffron explained.

"Oh," I said. It was a bit disappointing not to have the whole family present for the show, but if those were Viol's limits, I'd respect them. I wondered if his turbulent history had something to do with humans.

Suddenly, Aurum and Saffron's eyes went wide, as if noticing something behind me. A second later, I heard Vani's raspy voice call out, "Yo, Q!"

I turned around just in time to see him and Keaux running towards me. Anxious joy swirled in my chest. I was happy to see them, but it had been so long since we met in person. Jade arranged their visit for tonight's performance, and Vani and Keaux accepted.

It turned out I was nervous for nothing. My old friends slammed into me in a big group hug. Their embraces and familiar scents calmed my nerves.

"It's so good to see you, dude," Keaux said, wearing his usual lopsided grin.

"You guys, too," I said, meaning it. "By the way, nice rings."

They both blushed. The matching gold bands on their fingers shone bright, reflecting the stage lighting.

"Enough about us," Vani said. "Where's your man?"

"He's on standby," I said. "I want everything to be ready before we call him down."

Keaux leaned in, speaking in a conspiratorial whisper. "Is he *really* a dragon?"

"Yes," I said in a matching stage whisper. Pointing my thumb over my shoulder, I added, "All those guys are dragons. Well, except Taylor. He's a tiger."

Vani and Keaux blinked.

"Weird," Vani said. "You'd never know they weren't normal—er, regular humans."

"We can all hear you, you know," Crimson pointed out dryly.

Vani ducked his head as if Crimson would transform and cook him in a blast of fire. He cleared his throat. "Anyway, are we getting this show on the road or what?"

Keaux twirled his drum sticks. "Yeah, I'm itching to get on stage."

"Me, too," I agreed. Turning around to face my family, I took a deep breath. "Okay. We're ready. Would somebody go grab Thystle?"

Saffron shifted into dragon form before anyone else could offer. "I've got it!" he called from halfway into the sky. Meanwhile, Vani and Keaux looked like they'd just seen a UFO.

"I told you dragons were real," I teased.

By the time Saffron arrived with a blindfolded Thystle in tow, the rest of us were already on stage. My heart pounded when I saw my mate. He wore a grumpy yet curious expression. I could tell he wanted to see the big surprise, but didn't love the fact that his younger brother robbed him of his sight and manhandled him all the way to the beach.

Since Thystle couldn't see, Saffron took the liberty of holding Heather, so he was really only half paying attention to where he guided Thystle. Well, maybe more than half. Most of Saffron's attention was on the baby, cooing and making kissy faces at them. It was adorable—even when Saffron accidentally led Thystle into a big rock.

"Ow," Thystle mumbled.

"Oh, sorry," Saffron said, still smiling at Heather.

Sensing imminent disaster, the rest of Thystle's brothers arrived to take care of him. Crimson and Jade ushered him closer to the stage. Meanwhile, Aurum went and fetched Cobalt. Taylor smiled reassuringly at me while Ruby fussed in his arms. Everybody was present except Viol.

Or, that was what I thought—until he manifested out of nowhere behind everybody else. Dressed in all black leather, he looked like a walking shadow.

"Who's the biker daddy?" Keaux asked.

Just as he spoke, Viol shot the world's nastiest glare in his direction. Keaux paled and clutched his drum sticks tighter.

"That's my brother-in-law," I explained simply.

I was surprised to see Viol here after what Aurum said, but Viol's body language indicated he wasn't sticking around. He approached Taylor, tapped him on the shoulder, muttering something I couldn't hear. A moment later, Taylor smiled, nodded, and handed Ruby to him.

The second Viol held the infant, his whole demeanor changed. A radiant, genuine smile spread over his face. It warmed my heart to see him that happy since I'd met him.

With Ruby squared away in his muscular arms, Viol

went over to Saffron. I managed to overhear the conversation this time.

"It's going to be too loud for the kid," Viol explained. "Hand 'em over."

Saffron frowned, holding Heather closer. "What? No, it's my baby time."

Thystle, who was still blindfolded, mumbled, "Are you two fighting over *my* kid?"

"No one's fighting," Viol stated gruffly, "because Saffron is going to give Heather to me, and we're going to enjoy a nice, quiet nap."

"What, is there gonna be fireworks or something?" Thystle asked.

"The noise will be too much for infant ears," Viol growled, glaring daggers at Saffron.

Shockingly, Saffron glared back. Despite being related, they couldn't have looked more different. Saffron's small, bright appearance clashed with Viol's dark, domineering one. But they had one important thing in common—they both wanted to hold the baby.

I sighed. "Dragons."

In the end, Saffron agreed about the impending noise and handed Heather to Viol. With both babies tucked into his arms, he swaggered off to a quieter location. If it was anybody else in the world walking away with my child, I would've flipped my lid, but I trusted Thystle's family with all my soul. They were all incredibly caring uncles, especially Viol.

It was finally time. As I stepped up to the mic, everyone quieted down. It was no sold-out concert hall, but seeing every member of our little family gathered on the beach filled me to the brim with joy.

"Is anyone gonna tell me what's going on?" Thystle demanded.

I chuckled. "You can remove the blindfold now."

As soon as Thystle tore it off, his eyes widened and his jaw dropped. His brain seemed to short-circuit as he registered what was going on. His gaze snapped from me, to Vani and Keaux, to the speakers on stage, then back to me.

"You... wait, wait, wait," Thystle blurted, getting amped up. "What the hell's happening?"

My heart swirled in my chest as I brought the mic to my lips.

"Thystle Chromatimaeus," I said. "You probably know this already, but you're my world. If it weren't for you, I wouldn't be standing here on stage with my former band mates, ready to give you a one-of-a-kind TalonStorm concert."

Emotion wavered on Thystle's face as he stared at me, his amethyst eyes full of stars.

"One-of-a-kind?" he asked softly.

I nodded. "The big surprise I was working on is a new song. Just for you."

Thystle swayed from glee. He grabbed his closest brothers for support, clamping on to Jade and Saffron's arms like he'd pass out without them.

"Holy fucking Drake, is this real?" Thystle whimpered. "Am I high right now? Am I dead?"

Crimson rolled his eyes. "Oh, please. And people think *I'm* dramatic."

"Even Vani and Keaux are here," Thystle said shakily in awe. "Holy shit. You guys let them come? Just for this?"

Jade smiled. "It wouldn't be a true TalonStorm event without them."

Thystle looked like he was about to burst into tears, or scream, or faint. Maybe all three.

Before my mate went unconscious, I gripped the mic

and said, "Let's go, everyone. Here's our brand new single, *Amethyst Heart.*"

On my word, decorative fog rolled out behind the set. The stage lights darkened into a single spotlight that beamed onto the stage. I didn't have to cue my old friends. Vani and Keaux knew exactly what to do. They eased into the track like they'd played it a thousand times, even though it was brand new. They must've practiced after I sent them the vocals and chords. They'd done it for me —for *us.*

I shut my eyes as I felt the spotlight rain down on me.

Aquila took over. Frantic energy rocketed through my veins as I sang the first line. I fell into a trance, thinking only of my heartfelt performance, feeling the song in the marrow of my bones.

It was a song wholly dedicated to Thystle—my alpha, my love, the father of my child, my fated mate.

As I sang my heart out, I locked eyes with him. The love flowing between our gazes was magnetic. I needed him on stage with me.

I kneeled over the front ledge and held out my hand. Thystle grabbed it and leapt on. His eyes were brighter than any flame, shining with pure elation.

The vibration of the drums and guitar shook the stage. The song pounded through our blood, humming like a living thing. The whole moment felt surreal, dreamlike. It was perfect.

When the song was over, the roar of the crowd exploded. I was drenched in sweat, and so was Thystle, but neither of us cared. We slammed together in a warm embrace. I felt his heart thudding wildly through his chest, and I knew he felt mine doing the same.

"I love you," Thystle breathed, pressing his forehead to mine.

Warmth flooded my chest. "I love you, too."

He panted hard. "Kiss me, Aquila."

A shiver rolled across my skin. I grabbed Thystle, dipping him low as I crushed our mouths together in a hot, passionate kiss. Everybody went wild—our family, Vani and Keaux, Gaius, and even the stage helpers.

After we parted, Thystle stared up at me fondly, like I was the only person in the world.

"Can I get an encore?" he asked.

"Of the song, or the kiss?"

He shot me a sly, draconic grin. "Both."

I laughed. "Anything for you, my number one fan."

TWENTY-SIX

Epilogue: Thystle

THE NEXT MORNING, my eyes opened blearily to the sun's rays on my face. I barely remembered anything that happened after the end of the concert, except that Matteo and I had a fuckton of post-concert sex. It was a perfect night, and the most amazing gift he could've ever given me, aside from birthing our child.

Our child.

Heather.

I bolted up out of bed—which, I realized quickly, wasn't the bed, but the floor. Matteo was sprawled next to me in a messy pile of pillows and blankets. We must've ended up there during our rowdy escapades.

"Matteo," I blurted, shaking his shoulder.

He mumbled incoherently. He must've still been exhausted from the concert, plus the mind-blowing rounds of fucking. But I knew an instant way to wake him up.

"Where's Heather?" I asked.

Sucking in a sharp breath, Matteo sprang to consciousness. His hair looked like a bird's nest. I would've found it hilarious if I wasn't worried about my kid.

Matteo glanced around the room. "Gods. Did we

forget them?" Then his shoulders relaxed, as if he'd remembered something. "Oh, right. Heather is with Viol."

"You're more relaxed about that than I am," I grumbled, standing up and throwing clothes on in a hurry.

Matteo was nonplussed, but he slowly rose to dress himself. "Why wouldn't I be? He's a fantastic uncle. You brothers always fuss about him more than me and Taylor."

I made a face, but I couldn't argue. For some reason, Viol *did* get along better with the omegas than us, his literal flesh-and-blood brothers.

"It's because you're all so scared of him," Matteo mused, giving me a soft smile. "Why don't you treat him like any other family member?"

I crossed my arms. "I dunno. He's just...*Viol.* He's like the human personification of a rusty switchblade. One that stabs you in a dark alley."

Matteo snorted and arched a brow. "Okay, Thystle. Whatever you say. Shall we go retrieve our baby from this so-called rusty switchblade?"

"Please."

Just as we reached for the door to leave, it swung open. A glowering Viol stood before us. He always had bags under his eyes, but this morning they were darker than usual. I quickly realized why. Heather was fast asleep in his arms, looking cozy and comfortable wrapped up in a baby blanket. Our child must've kept Viol up all night. I couldn't stifle a laugh at the mental image of him trying—and probably failing—to wrangle an infant dragon.

"What's funny?" Viol grumbled.

I slapped a hand over my mouth. "Nothing."

Viol glared at me, but the hard edges of his face softened when he handed Heather to Matteo. My mate took them with a bright smile. Heather blinked their brown eyes open and yawned, flashing rows of little fangs. Fangs that no doubt chewed on Viol all night long.

"Good morning, sweetie," Matteo cooed. "Did you have fun with Uncle Viol?"

Heather let out a pleased draconic purr.

"I'll take that as a yes," Matteo said, smiling at Viol. "Thank you. It was a big help that you watched them overnight."

Viol almost looked uncomfortable at the praise. "No prob," he muttered. He shuffled his heavy-duty combat boots as if to leave, but paused to wriggle a finger at Heather. "See ya, kid."

He stalked off before either of us could respond.

"Seriously, how do you not think that's weird?" I whispered to Matteo.

"Oh, stop it. He's sweet."

I gasped and pressed my palm to his forehead. "Oh, no. Do you have a concussion from being in the mosh pit last night?"

Matteo grinned, swatting my hand away. "Okay, first of all, seven people does *not* constitute a mosh pit. Second, nobody even dropped me, so I'm fine. Third, you alpha dragons are the weird ones."

"Maybe," I conceded, grabbing his waist. "But you love it."

He sidled closer, a coy look in his eyes. "I do."

I leaned in to kiss him, but was cut off as Heather chomped on my shirt. Their eyes were bright and full of mischief, just like their papa.

"Looks like we just ruined all of Viol's hard work getting them to sleep," Matteo said with a laugh. "Now they're wide awake and hungry. Right, Heather?"

Our dragonet squawked like a demanding baby bird. Definitely awake and hungry.

I stole a quick kiss from Matteo's lips, not caring about the fact that my shirt had a big hole in it. "Sashimi breakfast?" I suggested.

Matteo chuckled, his gaze deeply fond. He carried Heather with one arm, and reached out for my hand with the other. "Mm. You know just what I like, my little fanboy."

"I *am* your number one fan, after all." I squeezed his hand tighter. "Always have been, always will be."

"I know," Matteo murmured, kissing me one last time before we headed downstairs hand-in-hand to where sushi trays awaited us.

THE END

Don't miss Cobalt's story in the next book: Alpha Dragon's Jackal!

Want to see Matteo's lullaby work its magic on Heather and dragons alike? Get the bonus scene by signing up to my newsletter!

Printed in Great Britain
by Amazon